QUEST FOR THE SPARK
BOOK THREE

WRITTEN BY **TOM SNIEGOSKI**

ILLUSTRATED BY **JEFF SMITH**

COLOR BY **STEVE HAMAKER**

An Imprint of

■ SCHOLASTIC

For Paul Deane —
One more time around the park.

Library of Congress Cataloging-in-Publication Data

Sniegoski, Tom.
Quest for the spark. Book 3 / written by Tom Sniegoski ; illustrated by Jeff Smith ; color by Steve Hamaker. – 1st ed.
p. cm. – (Bone)
Summary: As the evil Nacht spreads his darkness across the Valley, Tom and his friends, the Bone family, desperately try to find the Spark that will heal the Dreaming and save the world.
ISBN 978-0-545-14105-5
ISBN 978-0-545-14106-2 (paperback)
1. Adventure stories. 2. Quests (Expeditions) – Juvenile fiction. 3. Heroes – Juvenile fiction. 4. Dreams – Juvenile fiction. 5. Magic – Juvenile fiction. [1. Adventure and adventurers – Fiction. 2. Heroes – Fiction. 3. Dreams – Fiction. 4. Magic – Fiction. 5. Fantasy.] I. Smith, Jeff, ill. II. Hamaker, Steve. III. Title.
PZ7.S68033Quf 2013
813.6 – dc23
2012025128

ACKNOWLEDGMENTS
Cover and interior artwork by Jeff Smith
Text by Tom Sniegoski
Harvestar Family Crest designed by Charles Vess
Color by Steve Hamaker

10 9 8 7 6 5 4 3 2 1   13 14 15 16

First edition, February 2013
Edited by Cassandra Pelham
Book design by Phil Falco
Creative Director: David Saylor

Printed in China   38

Love and many thanks to my long-suffering wife, LeeAnne, for all that she does. Seriously, she makes me look good. And a special thanks to Kirby for giving me some pointers on how absolute evil should behave.

And always for Mulder.

Thanks also to Christopher Golden for being my sounding board, to Liesa Abrams and James Mignogna, Pete Donaldson, Dave and Kathy Kraus, Cassandra Pelham, David Saylor, Mom and Dad Sniegoski, Mom and Dad Fogg, Larry Johnson, Pat and Bob Dexter, Hadley, Max, Mel, Gava, Maxwell, and Timothy Cole and the Men of Pawa down at Cole's Comics in Lynn.

And, as always, a great big thank-you to Jeff and Vijaya for making me feel like part of the family.

Tom

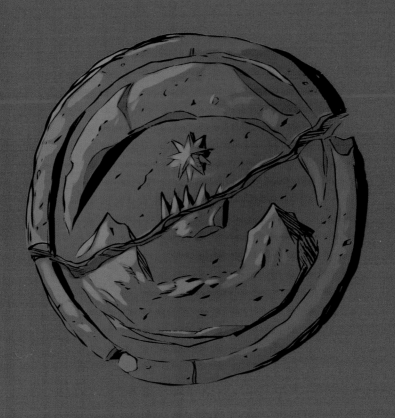

PROLOGUE

It was something he had always known might happen but had hoped wouldn't.

The Red Dragon tried to lift his mighty head, but it was far too heavy, still clogged with sleep. The Nacht was in control now, only allowing the Dragon an opportunity to open his eyes a crack to see the horrors the evil one had created.

To show off as he always had, even as a young Dragon so very long ago, before he'd escaped into the void between the Dreaming and the Waking World.

The Dreaming.

It saddened the Red Dragon to see what had been done to her, the darkness from the beyond now covering the once vibrant place with the stuff of shadow. And now that liquid blackness was spreading to the Waking World. He could hear the Nacht laughing as he towered above him.

"Do you see?" the black Dragon asked. "Do you see what I've done . . . what I'm about to do?"

"Make a very big mistake?" the Red Dragon said, his voice thick with sleep, slurring his words.

The Nacht laughed again. "No, not a mistake, brother," he answered. "But the fulfillment of my destiny."

The Red Dragon rolled his eyes. "Put me back to sleep if you're going to start shoveling that business."

The Nacht was suddenly in front of him, angry eyes glaring into his own.

"It has already begun," he declared. "Those with the strongest connection to the Dreaming were the first to fall. . . . I took them one after the other, cocooning them in a blanket of sleep and bringing them here."

The Nacht reared up on his thick back legs and spread his ebony wings. The surrounding gloom lifted like a fog to reveal the most nightmarish of visions.

As far as the Red Dragon could see were bodies, all caught in the grip of an endless sleep. Holy men lay scattered among the common folk of the Valley as royalty slumbered with Dragons — each and every one having fallen victim to the growing power of the Nacht. It was far worse than the Red Dragon could have ever imagined, but there was still a chance that the Nacht could be defeated.

For the Dreaming had seen this threat coming . . . and had planned.

"Your silence speaks volumes, brother," the Nacht growled happily as he walked past those who slept. He stopped before what appeared to be a curtain of absolute black. "Beyond this barrier is the prize," the Nacht purred. He raised a taloned hand and placed it against the obstruction. "The Waking World, just waiting for the darkness to flow over the land like an ocean."

The Dragon ran his razor-sharp claws along the shadow wall, slivers of night raining down to be lost in the shadows at his feet. "Already the work has begun," he continued. "Little by little, piece by piece, the wall is coming down."

The Nacht laughed again, his insidious joy escorting his brother back into the embrace of oblivion.

The last thought to go through the Red Dragon's mind before sleep claimed him once more was of one remaining chance for this nightmare to end.

The spark of a chance.

For from a spark, there often came fire.

· · ·

Porter slept beneath the cool, damp earth, head and legs tucked inside his shell, dreaming of friends who had come and gone throughout the long years he had lived. The memories were like a toasty fire, keeping the old turtle warm as he hibernated beneath the forest where he had lived his many days.

And that fire was growing — the recollections brighter and more intense than they had been for a very long time, slowly rousing him from his slumber.

Eyes fluttering open, the turtle poked his head from his shell, extended his legs, and started to crawl through the dirt toward the surface. He remembered what Stillman had told him as the friends said their good-byes.

"There might come a time when we're needed for a very important job."

"How will we know?" Porter asked.

"You'll know," Stillman replied as he'd walked toward the lake where he planned to sleep. *"The Dreaming will show you."*

Looks like Stillman was right, Porter thought, crawling up from the dirt. He brushed himself off and checked out his surroundings. Not much had changed in the forest swamp since he'd dug beneath the mud to sleep.

Or had it?

He felt it then, a kind of wrongness in the air — an icy chill that was the exact opposite of the warmth that had roused him from his slumber. This must be exactly what Stillman had warned him about.

Without further hesitation, the old turtle started through the woods, making his way toward the lake where his friend was likely still fast asleep.

Porter had a job to do.

He had a Dragon to wake.

Chapter 1

Tom Elm knew that he had to sleep, but it wasn't going to be easy.

He pulled a blanket tighter around his shoulders as he restlessly dozed in the belly of the *Queen of the Sky*.

Things out in the Valley had become bad.

While looking for supplies, they'd found another village, everyone in it held in the grip of nightmare.

It was some of the scariest stuff that Tom had ever seen, and what made it even scarier was that he knew it was going to get worse.

The Nacht was getting stronger, reaching out and snatching people — *whole villages* — from the Waking World, and from that he was growing more and more powerful.

Tom moaned as he lay somewhere between being awake and asleep. Thoughts of all he had been through on his quest to find the remaining pieces of the Spark, the now fragmented first ray of light that chased away the darkness so long ago, drifted through his mind. At first, he had been tormented by doubt, certain that the Dreaming had made a big mistake in choosing him as her champion, but now he could see how far he had come, how successful he had been. Maybe he wouldn't be a complete failure after all.

In that in-between place, he suddenly heard the words of his father, as he explained his philosophy about turnip farming.

"Never go into an endeavor uncommitted," Tom recalled him saying one evening as they ate their supper. *"You either go in to do that job to the fullest of your abilities, or you don't bother. Why waste the time if you're not going to give it your all?"*

Truer words had never been spoken, even though his father was talking about something completely different from saving the world from an evil Dragon.

Remembering his father's words made Tom think of his mom and little sister, too, and how they had all been victims of the Nacht's power. If he ever hoped to see them awake again, he had no choice but to give this his all.

He just hoped that he was strong enough for the job.

Sleep was gone, and Tom found himself suddenly very awake. Eyes adjusting to the shadows, he looked around to see where the others of the quest were. It had been raining on the deck above, so they had all come below to sleep. The Bone twins, Abbey and Barclay, lay snuggled up next to each other. Tom was amused to see them this way — normally they were punching, kicking, or otherwise tormenting each other. Beside them, curled up in a tight ball, was Roderick. The three of them had become quite close. Tom turned his head to see Randolf sitting, his back against the wall of the ship, arms folded. At first glance the Veni Yan warrior looked as though he was awake, but as Tom listened closely, he could hear the older man's slow, rhythmic breathing.

He glanced down at the strange stone that hung around his neck from a leather thong. The piece of the Spark was glowing softly, getting brighter and more insistent as the seconds passed.

Tom gulped, knowing what it meant. The Spark had something that it wanted to show him.

A vision.

A vision of the future.

Night had come far too quickly.

Chief Gnod of the Nurdak tribe, living within the far reaches of the rocky Southern Pawa region, sat upon his heavy throne of carved wood and waited uneasily for the screams to come.

He ran thick fingers through his long, graying beard, ears attuned to the sounds coming from outside his cabin.

The winds howled mournfully, as if aware of what was likely to come this night.

It had been two nights since the last attacks. Would there be a third?

A rhythmic pounding on the heavy wooden doors made him gasp and set the two hounds that rested on the floor at his feet to barking.

"Come!" the Chief bellowed as the doors leading into his quarters creaked open with a blast of freezing wind.

A slight, hooded figure floated in as if carried by the harsh breeze. Gnod scowled with disapproval.

"You were supposed to stay indoors with your mother," he said as his daughter removed her hood to expose pale, delicate features.

"I couldn't bear the thought of you in here alone," Gerta said.

"I am not alone," the Chief said, reaching down to pet the two faithful beasts. "Grimly and Boon are here with me."

Gerta knelt to pat the two fearsome-looking hounds, who lovingly licked her hands.

"It is quiet out there tonight, Father," the girl said. "Perhaps it is over —"

"Silence! Do not talk of it," the old Chief snapped. He looked around, waiting for the sounds of terror that had, as of late, come in the night.

The Chief believed he knew why his people were being

attacked. It was a curse of some kind, a curse from some higher power for following the desires of the Hooded One against the Kingdom of Atheia.

They were being punished for their brazen acts of war.

Punished by creatures that descended from the nighttime sky to steal away his subjects, carrying them up into the mountain caves, their screams fading off into the darkness.

"But it has been three nights, counting this one," Gerta said, coming to stand beside him.

Chief Gnod sat, listening. "The night is not yet over."

"But do you not think we have been punished enough?" she asked him.

"What I believe does not matter," the old Chief said. "It is how the powers that surround us feel."

"Then I think the powers are horrible and mean," the young girl said, clenching her fists.

Chief Gnod recoiled at his daughter's disrespectful words. If the powers that be were listening . . .

"Apologize!" he ordered, rising up from his chair. The hounds rose as well, watching the old ruler.

"I won't." Gerta stomped her foot. "And besides, even if I were to apologize, who would it be to?"

Chief Gnod's eyes were wide as he listened to the howling winds outside.

"You speak blasphemy. Offend the gods and our torment will go on and on."

"Do you know what I believe?" she asked defiantly. "I don't believe this has anything to do with what we've done."

"Stop!" the Chief commanded. "I will hear no more of this!"

"I have climbed some of the higher peaks of Pawa and have seen the darkness that is spreading, not only here . . . but also over the entire Valley."

The dogs began to whine, sniffing at the air.

"Now you've done it," the Chief growled, hand falling to the sword he wore at his side.

"I've done no such thing," Gerta said, but there was uncertainty in her voice.

Then they heard the sounds.

They were soft at first, mixing with those of the cold winds coming down from the mountains, and grew steadily louder.

"Do you see?" the Chief asked his daughter, reaching out to pull her protectively to him.

The heavy pounding of leathery wings could be heard from outside as Grimly and Boon began to growl, snapping ferociously at the air.

Chief Gnod pulled his daughter closer as the sounds intensified — the flapping of wings and the plaintive screams of those snatched up and stolen from their homes.

. . .

Tom slowly climbed the stairs from the hold onto the deck of the *Queen of the Sky*, the blistering effect of the Spark's latest vision still burning inside his brain.

What did it mean?

He hoped that the fresh air might help clear his head. The rain had stopped, leaving the deck shiny and slick, and the sun was trying to peek out from behind an assault of heavy, dark clouds. In his mind's eye, he again saw the image of solidified light, like a piece of jagged crystal, spinning in the darkness. The final piece that remained to be found before the Spark was complete.

The scenes that followed were like physical blows striking his head. Tom saw them in flashes: the *Queen of the Sky* in distress, Percival — the captain of the craft — trying to keep the sky ship from falling . . .

"Hey, Tom, you okay?" somebody asked him.

Tom turned to see that Percival had poked his head out of the wheelhouse.

"You don't look so good," the Bone explorer called. "You almost look as white as me . . . and that's pretty white."

"I'm fine," Tom said, unconvinced by his own words. The next image was of a fearsome-looking people — *warriors* — clothed in heavy furs, their hands clutching battle-worn weaponry.

He heard the sounds of thumping feet and turned to

see Barclay, Abbey, and Randolf emerging from below deck, concern on their faces.

"Is everything all right?" Randolf asked.

"Was that you screaming, Tom?" Barclay asked.

"You scared the heck out of me," Abbey Bone exclaimed.

As Tom faded in and out, he saw big, black creatures flying down from the sky, their eyes glowing red and mouths filled with razor-sharp teeth. . . .

"What is wrong, Tom?" the Veni Yan asked as he gripped Tom's shoulder, freeing him from his vision.

Tom didn't want to worry them. "It's all right," he managed. He even tried to smile, but it was short lived. "The latest vision . . . I . . . I don't understand what . . ."

Aside from the horrible fanged things of darkness, he saw what could only be described as a giant cat, an enormous lion of some kind stalking the mountains of the north.

"What did you see, Tom?" Percival asked. "Is . . . is it that bad?" The Bone was nervous, and Tom couldn't blame him.

"A giant cat," Tom said cautiously. "I think we're supposed to find him."

He didn't want to tell them about the other things he'd seen . . . the more disturbing things.

"Roque Ja," the Veni Yan said with understanding. "You're talking about the beast called Roque Ja."

The two Rats emerged from beneath a heavy tarp, where they had hidden to protect themselves from the rain.

"Did somebody say Rock Jaw?" Stinky asked.

"Please say that you didn't," begged Smelly. "Please have it be anything but that."

"Well, it's pretty hard to mistake Rock Jaw for something else," Stinky said. "Rock Jaw . . . yep, can't really think of anything else that sounds like . . ."

The Rats continued their banter, but Tom's attention had already started to shift back to the memories of his vision.

He was in a cave, descending deeper and deeper.

A wall was suddenly before him, something scratching on the other side of it, picking away at the obstruction until —

"Is he well?" someone asked, and Tom turned to find one of the stranger members of their quest. Lorimar stood before him, her spirit housed in a body formed from the seed of a mighty oak tree.

Tom's mouth opened at the sight of her, remembering something else the Spark had shown him — the most disturbing vision of them all.

Lorimar had been there, her body made up from some

strange form of plant life that glowed with an eerie incandescent light. Tom was on his knees, looking up at her. She was speaking, but for some reason he couldn't hear her.

His confusion grew as she picked him up and forced him at the wall. He barreled through it and into the darkness on the other side.

Where the Nacht was waiting.

Tom cried out in fear and panic.

"There he goes again," Abbey Bone said.

Tom was about to tell his friends that it was okay, that he was fine. But he never got the chance.

He passed out before the words could leave his mouth.

CHAPTER 2

Percival watched from the wheelhouse of the *Queen of the Sky* as Tom went down like a sack of bricks, both hands firmly gripping the sky craft's wheel. The storm had passed, but the wind was something awful.

"Is he okay?" the Bone explorer shouted.

"It appears the Dreaming's latest vision was quite hard on the lad," Randolf informed. "But I believe he'll be all right."

That made Percival feel better . . . until he saw what they were about to fly into. The winds coming off the Northern Mountains were dangerous, like eager hands ready to grab hold of the *Queen* and dash her on the cold, rocky peaks below. He needed both hands to keep the *Queen* on course.

"How's it going back there?" Percival asked, trying to keep the nervousness from his voice.

"Tom's fine," his niece, Abbey, answered. "I think he

was probably just hungry. You know what they say about having visions on an empty stomach."

"Not really," Percival answered as the wheel began to struggle in his grasp. "But I'll take your word for it."

Thick, billowing clouds that formed around the higher mountain peaks had created a kind of barrier up in front of them, like a really bad fog bank rolling in their direction. Percival didn't like it, not one little bit. There was nothing worse than not being able to see where you're going, especially in the vicinity of a mountain range.

"Hey, guys, you might want to hold on to something," Percival called out from the wheelhouse. "Things could get a little rough."

The clouds enveloped them, and the temperature seemed to drop twenty degrees. Immediately, Percival felt the wheel shaking so hard that he was afraid it might be torn from his grip.

"Uncle Percy?" he heard a small voice say.

Percival turned his head to see his nephew, Barclay, standing in the doorway of the wheelhouse.

"Do what I said," the Bone explorer cried, more frantically than he intended.

The little Bone looked terrified, and Percival wished with all his heart that he could have gone to the little boy, held him in his arms, and told him that everything was going to be all right.

But he couldn't do that at the moment — he had a ship to keep in the air.

And besides, he promised that he would never lie to his niece and nephew.

Tom awakened to chaos.

He quickly climbed to his feet, angry that he'd blacked out.

Randolf grabbed his arm to steady him, the Veni Yan's inquisitive stare connecting to his.

"I'm okay now, Randolf," he said, lurching across the deck as the *Queen of the Sky* rocked from side to side.

"What's happening?" Tom asked Percival as he held on to the door frame of the wheelhouse.

"Not sure," Percival answered. "These clouds are as thick as Granny Pinkerton Bone's ham-and-clam soup. . . . And the winds coming off these mountains — which I can't see by the way — aren't doing us much good, either."

Tom could see that the Bone was struggling to keep the craft under his control and remembered his vision of the *Queen of the Sky* in distress.

"Maybe we should put her down," Tom said.

"Great idea, but where?" Percival asked. "We can't see our hands in front of our faces."

Percival was right. The cloud bank was so thick that they were flying blind.

"What if we flew lower?" Tom suggested. "Got below the clouds."

Percival looked at him with worry in his tiny, dark eyes. "And risk running into a mountain? Don't think that would be wise."

The vision of the *Queen of the Sky* going down flashed in his mind again, but Tom refused to accept it. There had to be something they could do to navigate the clouds and land someplace safely.

Tom looked around to see the others frozen in place, watching to see what would happen next.

"I'm a little scared," Abbey Bone said, holding on to one of Randolf's legs.

"There's nothing to be a'scared of, right?" Barclay Bone asked. He moved over and grabbed on to Randolf's other leg.

"Then we'll go higher," Tom said, turning back to the wheelhouse. "We'll go straight up and hopefully get above the clouds without running into anything."

"You took the words right out of my mouth," Percival said, keeping the wheel steady with one hand. The chubby fingers of his other were already reaching for the controls that would allow the *Queen* to climb vertically and hopefully take them to some semblance of safety above the thick, dangerous clouds.

"Nothing to be afraid of," Tom said reassuringly to the twins, Roderick, Randolf, and Lorimar. The two Rats were peeking out from beneath the protection of the deck tarp.

He felt the *Queen* begin its ascent and started to believe that they had narrowly averted danger, when they all heard the sound. A roar, followed by the sound of something ripping and then a tremendous hiss.

The sound of escaping air.

"Something's happened to the balloons!" Percival screamed as the *Queen* began to drop.

The ship started to plummet. There was no doubt that something hidden by the clouds had attacked them. The image of the great mountain cat leaping at them from a rocky perch flashed before his mind's eye as the sky ship descended blindly, Percival's cries filling him with an unconscionable dread.

"Abandon ship," the Bone explorer bellowed. "We've got to abandon ship!"

In a cave beneath a lake, a tiny Dragon slept.

Stillman dreamed of the adventures he'd had protecting the young orphan animals of the forest from ending up in the bellies of the evil Rat Creatures, as their parents had.

In his dreams, he saw all their faces: Lily Bear, Pete Porcupine, Ramona Fox, and Porter Turtle, all of them having grown up strong and healthy and many even having families of their own.

A smile crept across the sleeping Dragon's face as he

remembered Big Johnson Bone and the world of trouble that he had caused the Rats.

It had been a good life, but now he was supposed to sleep — and wait.

At least that was what the Red Dragon told him to do.

Stillman dreamed of the day the Red Dragon had come to see him. He'd been surprised to see him, thinking almost at once that he'd done something wrong and that Red was there to take back the title of forest protector.

But the Red Dragon had been there for something else.

Something that might be important for the future.

"So you're not firing me from my job as forest protector?" Stillman asked, relieved that he hadn't done a bad enough job to get canned.

"Not at all," the Red Dragon said with a shake of his large head. "I've come to tell you about your new job."

"A new job?" Stillman asked, his heart leaping into his throat. "For me?"

The Red Dragon nodded. "The one you were born to do."

"But I thought that forest protector . . ."

"That was just a warm-up," the Dragon told him. "The Dreaming has bigger plans for you."

"The *Dreaming*?" Stillman asked, in an awe-filled whisper. "Imagine that."

The Red Dragon moved closer, slipping a powerful arm around Stillman's shoulder.

"The Dreaming needs you to be ready in case of a special emergency," the Dragon told him. "You and your fire."

"My fire?" Stillman asked incredulously. "But I couldn't even breathe fire without getting sick to my stomach until recently."

For a moment, Stillman considered that this was all some sort of joke, that the Red Dragon and his Dragon buddies were pulling a prank on him. But it was the look in Red's eyes that convinced him otherwise, a look that showed him that what the older Dragon was talking about was the furthest thing from a joke.

"That's because your fire is special, kid," the Red Dragon said. "And you couldn't let it out until it was ready."

Stillman let the Red Dragon's words slowly sink in.

"Is it ready now?" he asked. "Am *I* ready now?"

"The Dreaming and I believe that it is — and that you are," the Dragon said. "Almost."

"Almost? What do I need to do to . . ."

The old Dragon held out his hand, showing something to Stillman. At first it looked like a shiny rock, but upon closer examination it appeared to be something more.

So much more.

"What is it?" Stillman asked, reaching a tiny hand toward the object.

"Let's just say that it's something that will help you reach your full potential."

The strange stone pulsed with an eerie inner light, and Stillman could not help but be comforted by it.

"It's beautiful," the tiny Dragon said, unable to take his eyes from it. "Can I have it?" His hand hovered over the special stone.

"You can do even better than that," the Red Dragon said. "You can swallow it."

"Swallow it?" Stillman asked, the strange idea diverting his attention. "Why would I want to do something like that?"

The Red Dragon stared at him, wearing the most serious of expressions. "Because that's what the Dreaming and I need you to do."

"This will help me reach my full potential?" Stillman asked as he took the softly glowing stone from the Red Dragon's palm.

"It certainly will," Red answered, watching him closely.

Stillman looked at the stone, bringing it closer to his mouth. "So I should just gulp this down?" he asked nervously, stalling.

"You should," the old Dragon said with a nod. "That is, if you want to reach your full potential."

"Maybe I should get myself a glass of water so I don't choke and —"

"Down the hatch," the Red Dragon urged, pretending to swallow an imaginary stone.

Stillman studied the stone again, its gentle pulse of light somehow assuring him that he would be okay, that he wouldn't choke at all.

"Bombs away," the little Dragon said as he tossed the softly glowing rock into his maw and noisily gulped it down.

Glumph!

Stillman thought he might gag as the rough-edged stone slowly slid down his gullet, but any sign of discomfort was soon gone. The stone seemed to dissolve as it made its way into his belly.

"That'a boy," the Red Dragon praised.

Stillman could feel something unusual happening in

his belly, where his fire was made. It was almost as if the stone and his fire were mixing together, becoming something . . .

Different.

"It feels kinda funny," Stillman said, holding on to his slightly protruding middle.

"It should," Red said. "But now you're really ready."

Stillman had to admit he was a little bit nervous about this new responsibility being heaped upon him, but was also quite honored.

"So this new job," the little Dragon said, "what do I have to do?"

"That's what I like to hear," the Red Dragon said, slapping him roughly on the shoulder and almost knocking him down. "Always knew you were a go-getter."

"Thanks," Stillman said.

"But right now I need you to wait," the Red Dragon told him.

"How long?" Stillman asked.

The Red Dragon shrugged. "That I really don't know," he said. "Might be awhile, but if what the Dreaming suspects might happen happens . . ."

The Red Dragon's voice trailed off, and he grew very serious again, gazing off into the forest. He then went on to explain how a dark and evil force might try and bring total darkness to the Valley and then to the world outside. He described the part the little Dragon would play in all this and how very important it was.

"This special job," Stillman asked, still reeling, "will I have to do it alone?"

The Red Dragon slowly blinked his large eyes as he considered the question.

"No," the great Dragon said. "No, you won't."

This made Stillman feel a little bit better, remembering the help he'd had while defending the forest against the Rat Creatures.

The Red Dragon turned his massive bulk around and started walking away, deeper into the forest. Stillman just stood there, unsure of what he should be doing.

"Ummm," the little Dragon began. "Sir? What should I be doing?"

"Nothing right now," the Red Dragon answered, not even turning around. "It could be a while. Maybe a long while. You should probably think about taking a nap — rest up for what might be coming."

"Okay," Stillman said, rubbing his little hands together. "And my help? Who is going to help me?"

The Red Dragon stopped and turned his head.

"You got a best friend, right?" he asked.

Stillman nodded. "Yes, sir, his name is Porter."

"Porter," the Red Dragon repeated. "He's a turtle, isn't he?"

"Yes, sir."

"Turtles are perfect," the Dragon stated. "They live a good long time. He'll be helping you out . . . waking you up when it's time."

The Red Dragon turned away from him again and sauntered off into the expanding shadows of the forest, his thick tail dragging behind him.

"I won't let you down, sir!" Stillman called.

"Let's hope that you don't," he answered. "For all our sakes."

Stillman stirred as he again dreamed of that special day. Not long after his special purpose was revealed to him, he found his best friend and explained what the Red Dragon had told him. Porter was frightened by this new responsibility, but the two friends had been through quite a lot together over the years Stillman was a forest protector. The little Dragon explained that this was a special extension of that.

With Porter finally agreeing to help him, Stillman said good-bye to his best friend, reminding the turtle to wake him up when it was time. Then he dove into the lake and found himself a nice little air-filled cave beneath the waters to curl up in and catch a snooze.

And to wait.

Stillman didn't think he'd been asleep all that long before feeling himself being shaken awake. Bleary-eyed, the little Dragon awakened to see his friend Porter standing over him.

"What is it, buddy?" Stillman asked, rubbing sleep from his eyes.

"You gotta wake up," the little turtle said to him. "I had a crazy dream."

And that was when the Dragon noticed how much older his friend looked, as if a lot of time might've passed by.

"You mean it's time?" Stillman asked, feeling his tiny heartbeat flutter, and the fire — *the special fire* — in his belly start to burn.

Porter nodded his little turtle head up and down.

"I think it is."

CHAPTER 3

The situation was bad . . . really bad.

Percival could see that at least two of the three balloons had been torn, flapping, jagged rips spewing the hot gas needed to keep the *Queen* afloat.

They were going down whether they wanted to or not.

The clouds had cleared enough that he could see the mountains — hard, cold, and rocky — quickly coming up beneath them, and there wasn't a chance in heck that they wouldn't hit at least one of them on the way down.

As much as it pained him to make the decision, there was only one thing they could do.

"Abandon ship!" he cried, still holding tight to the wheel as the *Queen of the Sky* began to fall.

Percival hoped that there was enough time. If he was going to get everybody off the *Queen* before they collided with one of the mountains, he was going to have to move fast.

The Bone explorer stepped back from the wheel and reached down to a series of cabinets beneath the control panel.

Tom was frantic. "Percival, what should we —"

"Not now, Tom," Percival said. He quickly undid the metal straps that held the cabinets closed and pulled out rescue harnesses that he had stored in case of such an emergency. After their last crash landing, he'd been working many late nights to get this particular invention into working order.

And at this moment, he was glad that he did. But there were only four harnesses, so they would need to make do.

"Here," Percival said to everyone standing outside of the wheelhouse. "Put these on."

"Do we really gotta abandon ship?" Abbey asked, on the verge of tears.

He first gave one to Tom, then Abbey, Barclay, and Randolf.

"What is this?" the Veni Yan priest asked, examining the harness, which had a pouchlike object attached.

"Don't ask questions, just put it on," Percival ordered. He glanced out to the front of the ship, the anticipation making him feel as though he had fifty thousand volts of electricity passing through him. "Make sure that pouch is at your back."

He watched as Tom slid his arms through the straps.

"C'mon, c'mon," Percival rushed them.

Barclay and Abbey were the first to finish — having seen this invention in its earliest stages — and then helped Randolf with his harness.

"Where's mine?" asked a voice at his side.

Percival looked over to see a frightened raccoon rubbing his little paws together.

"You're with us," Abbey told Roderick, pulling him over to stand beside her and Barclay.

"Where's yours?" Tom asked Percival as he made sure the straps on his harness were tight.

Percival ignored the question and looked at Lorimar, who stood gazing out over the side of the falling ship as if she didn't have a care.

"You!" Percival called.

The tree woman turned her leafy gaze toward him.

"I'm guessing you can take care of yourself," he told her.

Lorimar nodded, and then, suddenly, her body broke apart, dried bark and leaves landing on the deck to be blown about by the wind.

"Figured as much," Percival said.

"Wait," Tom said, grabbing his arm. "I asked you a question."

"A captain always goes down with his ship," the Bone said, pulling his arm away.

The Rats had emerged from beneath the safety of their tarp.

"Fredrick and I aren't captains," Stinky said, waving his dead squirrel around. "And we've never wanted to be."

"Me neither," Smelly added. "It's the whole going-down-with-the-ship thing that really doesn't work for me."

"I'm sorry, but I don't have enough harnesses to go around, and besides, there's a weight limit, and you two would be too heavy. You're going to have to take your chances with me," Percival said, pointing at the two beasts. "Get below deck before . . ."

Through the shifting clouds, the Bone explorer caught a glimpse of glistening wet rock coming up on them quickly, which told him that they were close.

Very close.

"Go!" Percival cried, dashing over to the four wearing the special harnesses. He reached out and grabbed hold of a dangling tab that hung from one of Tom's straps and gave it a yank.

"You can't stay on the *Queen* if she's —" The pouch on Tom's back exploded open, and a large, gas-filled balloon instantly inflated to full size, lifting the boy from the deck and up into the clouds before he could finish.

Percival reached for the twins next.

"No!" Abbey shrieked, jumping back from her uncle's hands. "If you're not going, neither am I!"

"Abbey, please," Percival said. This would be hard enough without her fighting him.

"I'm not going either," Barclay declared.

Their time was running out, and he knew how stubborn the twins could be. He needed to think fast.

"So it's mutiny, is it?" Percival stumbled back, hand clutched to his chest. "I never would've imagined such a thing from a crew so loyal, but I guess I was wrong."

"No, no, Uncle Percival," Barclay said. "We're not mutinying, we just don't want to leave you with the *Queen* going down and all."

"Not mutinying?" Percival asked. "But in not leaving, you're disobeying a direct order from your captain."

"But we don't want to leave you!" Abbey cried, huge tears dribbling down her chubby cheeks.

"But you don't want to be mutineers either," Roderick said, looking at the twins. "Right?"

It took a moment, but Percival could see that his idea, with Roderick's assistance, had worked. If there was anything that the twins took seriously, it was the laws of the ship.

Abbey grabbed hold of her raccoon friend and held him tight.

"There's a good crew," Percival said with relief. "I promise that I'll do everything in my power to bring her down safely."

"We love you, Uncle Percy," the twins said in unison, tears streaming down their faces as they pulled their own tags and floated from the deck.

"See ya below!" Roderick called out.

"Be brave," Randolf said as he hesitantly reached for the tag on his harness.

"Right back at'cha," Percival said, beating the warrior priest to the punch and giving the tag to inflate his balloon a sharp tug.

Worked like a charm, the Bone thought as he watched Randolf lift from the deck and drift away on the wind to relative safety along with the others.

He turned to see the Rats crammed into the wheelhouse doorway, their eyes huge with fear.

"Get below," Percival commanded, launching himself across the deck. He pushed the two furry monsters aside and took hold of the wheel.

A wall of ice-encrusted rock materialized through a new bank of shifting clouds, and he spun the wheel severely to try and avoid it.

The sound of rock scraping across wood was one of the most unpleasant sounds he had ever heard.

That and the sound of the Rats screaming as a mountain appeared in front of them.

"Not good," Percival said, unable to tear his eyes from the sight. "Not good at all."

• • •

Lorimar allowed her current body formed from the seed of
an oak to fall apart, leaving the deck of the flying ship, to
reform somewhere in the mountains below.

But something happened as she attempted to do this.

Something pulled her spirit to a place between here and there. A place she had been before, where she learned something that had changed her world.

The darkness surrounded her like the ocean, threatening to crush her in its all-encompassing blackness, but a single dot of light gave her the strength to move toward the warm glow in the icy-cold sea of pitch.

A bubble of untainted Dreaming hovered in the realm of shadows, and within it, Lorimar could see a piece of what once was.

What she believed was gone forever.

More of the First Folk — her brothers and sisters — peered out from within the bubble, a piece of the Dreaming saved especially for them to survive.

Especially for her.

The Nacht had done this. The Dragon of darkness had told her so when she was last here.

It was as if the very thought summoned him; the black Dragon seemingly forming from the sea of ebony around her, looming above the fragile bubble that contained everything that she had ever loved and believed lost.

"I thought you should see them again," the Nacht growled. "To remind you of what you will lose lest you forget our arrangement."

Lorimar hadn't forgotten — in fact, it was all that had occupied her thoughts since returning to her friends who quested for the Spark. The Nacht wanted her to betray the heroes . . . those who the Dreaming had chosen to find the first light of creation to drive back the darkness once again.

"I . . . I haven't forgotten," she stammered.

"Then you remember what I want," the great beast purred. He wrapped his large, clawed hands around the globe, holding it like a child would a ball. "What I must have in order to give you what you most long for."

Lorimar remained silent, staring at her people, who cowered within the transparent globe.

"Remind me of my desire," the Nacht snarled. "Refresh my memory."

The Dragon began to squeeze, and the magical bubble cracked like an egg beneath the pressure. The First Folk within cried out in terror.

"Tell me," the Nacht commanded.

"Stop!" Lorimar begged. "The Spark. . . . You want the Spark."

"And you will bring it to me once it has been reformed," the Dragon added.

"I will bring it to you."

"Excellent," the Nacht said, growing even larger before her eyes, now holding the bubble of the Dreaming like a pebble in the palm of its clawed hand. Making sure that she was watching, the Nacht tossed the sphere into his cavernous mouth and swallowed.

Lorimar looked on in petrified silence.

"For safe keeping," the black Dragon told her. "Now go and bring the Spark to me."

And as suddenly as he appeared, the Nacht was gone.

The *Queen* disappeared beneath Tom's feet as the balloon on his back yanked him up into the murky sky. He watched in disbelief as the sky ship continued its descent without him and could see that two of the *Queen*'s balloons were torn, the rips in the heavy material flapping like eager mouths. A single balloon was all that kept the great ship from falling like a stone, but it could only do so much.

He cried out to the others, the sound of his voice lost in the howl of the winds. One by one he watched his friends fly from the deck of the ship as the *Queen of the Sky* was swallowed up by the roiling black clouds.

Tom wiggled his feet and kicked his legs, throwing the weight of his body forward in an attempt to push himself in the direction the *Queen* and his friends had gone, but it was to no avail. He was helpless, drifting without control and worried that whatever had torn the *Queen*'s balloons might decide to come for him, too.

The mountain winds attacked him, tearing at his

clothes and pulling at the balloon that held him afloat, drawing him down through the thick, shifting clouds — to where, he did not know.

His thoughts raced. *What will happen now? Without the Queen? Without my friends?*

Will there even be a quest now?

What will happen to the Valley? To the world?

It was too much for him to bear. He wanted to scream out in frustration — angry at the blinding clouds, angry at whatever it was that had attacked the *Queen*, angry at the Dreaming for picking someone who wasn't good enough for such an important job.

Just then, the rough, rocky surface of a mountain range appeared dramatically from the shifting mist, and the ground rushed up to meet him. Tom could do nothing but hold tightly to the straps beneath his arms as the ground drew closer, bracing for the inevitable.

Maybe this is it, he thought just before impact.

Maybe this is the day that I die.

The Chief accompanied the hunting party out into the hills on their search for sustenance.

Meat had been scarce in these parts since the skies above their land had filled with the strange, smokelike clouds that blotted out the sun, bringing an eerie twilight to everything below.

His people were afraid, and he knew that he must do everything in his power to reassure them that they would be fine.

That he would protect them.

He and the four others who made up the hunting party trudged over the rocky terrain, following the tracks of what looked to be some mountain goats. That alone was a promising sight, most of the wild goats in this region having long fled or become meals since the great cat of the mountains, Roque Ja, had started hunting in Pawa territory.

To be following this trail was a good sign . . . a sign that things might be returning to normal.

If only he could truly believe it.

The Chief squatted down, examining the rocky ground, searching for signs that the goats had passed, and found a patch of scrub growth that had been nibbled on.

"They've come this way," he announced, leaning on his staff to help him rise. He felt his old, tired bones creak and was glad that only he could notice the discomfort. He must never show the younger members of the hunting party signs of weakness, for it could lead to them challenging his Chiefdom.

And would that be such a bad thing? Gnod turned his gaze to the others — all fine, strong men who physically fit the part of ruler, but could they bear the heavy weight of the crown and all that it required?

No, this was his job, as it had been his father's, and his father's father's before him. He would see his people through this darkness.

A blast of icy wind whipped across the mountain, and Gnod glanced up into the cloud-filled sky, wondering when his people would again feel the warmth of the sun.

And, as if receiving some sort of sign in response to his question, the Chief watched something fall from the clouds. Another object was right behind it, floating down not far from where they stood.

"Did you see?" one of the hunters asked.

"I saw," the Chief answered.

"What . . . what was it?" another of the party asked fearfully. "Perhaps we should return to the village before . . ."

It made Gnod sad to see how the seeds of fear had taken root in their village's men since the nighttime attacks had begun.

"No," the Chief answered. "What if they were birds? Would we deny our people a chance for meat? No, we must go and see."

"But . . . but what if they're not birds?" one of the hunters asked. "What if they're . . . something else?"

"Then we'll just have to see," the Chief said sharply, turning his back on them and heading off across the rocky landscape.

It was not long before the others followed. As Gnod

suspected, the objects that fell were not far, and he held his staff tightly as he approached them.

They were not birds, of that he was certain.

"Careful, my Chief," one of his men cautioned as he slowly stalked closer to the first of the objects.

An object that was in fact a boy.

Gnod stood over the young man. There was a strange, bubblelike object attached to the youth that floated above his head. It darted and wove in the wind, and Chief Gnod leaned in closer, extending the point of his spear.

The bubble popped with a large clap, causing the Chief to leap back. It lay in tattered pieces on the ground now, the boy unconscious.

The other of the pair was the more unusual. Also unconscious, it appeared to be a boy as well, but a boy unlike any he had ever seen. His skin was pale white, and he had a large, round nose. Gnod wondered if this could be one of those Bone creatures he'd heard tell of, that were friends of the Atheians. The Bone, if that was what it was, was attached to one of the bubblelike things as well, but it had already been torn.

"What are they?" one of his men asked.

Gnod looked at him. "A boy . . . and what I think is a Bone," the Chief said, pointing to each with the tip of his staff.

"But they fell from the sky," the man added.

"Yes, they did," acknowledged the Chief.

"What if they're the ones that have been coming during the night?" the hunter went on.

The others grew agitated by the suggestion, gripping their weapons.

"Then we should strike them down before . . ." began another of the hunters, stepping forward with his spear raised over the unconscious boy.

"You'll do no such thing," the Chief commanded.

There was something about them, Gnod thought. Something that told him these two might be special.

"But what if . . . ?"

"Your Chief has made his decision," Gnod said with authority. He glared at them unblinkingly. "We'll take them back to the village. I would like to speak to them when they awaken, to learn of how they have come to fall from the sky."

CHAPTER 4

Stillman gazed up through the trees of the forest at the threatening sky. Though the sun still shone, wisps of black clouds were circling the brilliant orb. A foreboding chill ran down the length of the orange Dragon's spine to the tip of his chubby tail.

"Are you all right, Stillman?" Porter asked.

The little Dragon looked at his friend, who was standing beside him.

"I'm fine, just thinking about the job ahead of us."

The turtle brought a claw to his chin.

"Yeah, I was thinking about that, too," he said. "Tell me again why the Red Dragon said that I had to go?"

"Because you're my best friend, and you don't want me doing this alone, do you?" Stillman asked, hands on his hips.

"No, but you said the Red Dragon told you it would

be dangerous, and I'm not so sure how I'll do with danger these days," Porter said. "I am pretty old."

"You'll be fine," he said. "Remember, you'll be with me, the protector of the forest."

"But we won't be in the forest, will we?"

"Good point," Stillman said, rubbing his chin in thought. "But it really shouldn't matter. Once a protector, always a protector."

"If you say so," Porter said.

"And besides, I really appreciate the company."

The turtle thought a little more, then shrugged. "All right, I'll go. I wasn't planning on doing much more than sleeping in the mud anyway."

"That's the spirit," Stillman said, patting his friend's shell.

"So," Porter began. "Where are we going from here?"

"Good question," Stillman said.

The Dragon concentrated for a moment and felt the fire in his belly begin to bubble and roil, as if wanting to be freed. Remembering what the Red Dragon had said about his fire, and how it would be special, he tilted his head back and blew a stream of orange fire into the air.

"Wow!" Porter said. "Looks like you really got the hang of that."

The Dragon smiled. It had taken him a long time to be able to breathe fire correctly, and it felt good to let it out.

Stillman and Porter kept their eyes on the mass of fire that churned in the air until it started to take shape.

"What's it doing?" Porter asked, transfixed by the wondrous sight.

"I'm really not sure, but give it a sec," Stillman said. "The Red Dragon said that my fire was special, and then he made me eat a rock and —"

"He made you eat a rock?" Porter asked disbelievingly.

"Shush," Stillman told his friend, continuing to watch his fire. "The Red Dragon said that my fire would tell us where we needed to go."

Finally, Stillman's fire took the form of an arrow that pointed them in a northerly direction.

"Wow, would ya look at that?" Porter said, awestruck.

"Yeah, ain't it something? It looks like we're heading that way," the Dragon said, and he and his turtle friend started their journey . . . following an arrow of fire.

Percival knew he had to be dreaming.

He was standing on a stage, accepting a trophy from the Boneville Explorers' Society for being Boneville's explorer of the decade.

Flashbulbs were popping as photographers from the Boneville papers — the *Boneville Gazette* and the *Boneville Times* — took pictures for their front pages. The other members of the Explorers' Society had come onstage,

trying desperately to be in the pictures with him, proud that somebody of his caliber was a member of their illustrious group.

As the cameras flashed, the reporters shouted out questions, and patrons of the ceremony shoved pieces of paper at him for autographs. Percival was answering questions and signing his name when he got a sense of something . . . missing.

"Abbey?" he called out, trying to look over the heads of the reporters and his adoring public. "Barclay?"

But the twins were nowhere to be found.

Where are they? he asked himself.

Percival pushed his way through the crowd. *This isn't right*, he thought as he searched for his niece and nephew. They should be here with him.

And what happened to Tom, Roderick, Randolf, and Lorimar?

What happened to the Nacht?

He caught sight of the Rat Creatures at the back of the hall, dressed in fine tuxedoes, arguing back and forth as one attempted to straighten the bow tie of the other.

Big surprise.

Percival approached them, questions dancing on the tip of his tongue. Maybe these two would know where . . .

And then he caught pieces of their conversation, and he

realized that they were arguing about whether or not they should eat somebody.

About whether or not they should eat *him*.

And as the Bone explorer was about to tell them that they weren't going to be eating anybody, he realized that he'd turned into a giant bratwurst smothered in mustard.

Yep, it was a dream all right.

But even as he realized this and found himself slowly coming around, he could still hear the Rats going on and on about eating him.

"But he looks so delicious lying there all defenseless," Stinky said.

"I'm just not sure we should," Smelly responded.

"What if we just take a little bite?" Stinky suggested.

"Hmmm," Smelly contemplated. "How little is little?"

"Maybe an arm or a leg . . . depending on which one has the most meat on it."

"That could work," Smelly relented.

Percival got a sense that his time — and the Rats' self-control — might be running out. The Bone explorer came to with a grunt and a twitch, sitting up to see the two Rat Creatures leaning over him, thick dribbles of spit raining down from their mouths.

"Can I help you two with something?" Percival asked, rubbing the back of his neck and head. He must've bumped it pretty good.

The Rats were crouched on the steps in the wheelhouse that led down into the hold. They looked surprised to see him awake.

"Oh no, we're good," Stinky said, fanning himself with the ragged remains of his dead squirrel.

"We were just wondering if you were gonna wake up," Smelly quickly added.

"I bet you were." Percival gave them both the stink eye, knowing full well what they had been up to. But as his grandfather Ignatius Bone used to say, there's no sense in trying to convince a skunk not to smell bad.

"So how bad is it?" Percival asked, climbing slowly to his feet.

The wheelhouse didn't appear to be too damaged. There was a big crack in the window, but the controls seemed to be in good shape.

"We crashed," Smelly said.

"In the mountains," Stinky added.

"Tell me something I don't know," the Bone said, making his way toward the deck.

The *Queen* was tilted strangely to one side, and he had to walk at an odd angle in order to get to the ship's edge. He peered over the side. The hull looked as though it had some holes punched through it from the rocky landing, but it didn't appear to be anything that he couldn't patch up.

He leaned back to observe the balloons. It was as he'd

feared — they were completely deflated and torn up pretty badly. The propellers looked like they had taken a beating as well.

All in all, Percival believed everything could be fixed, but it wasn't going to be easy. He thought of the others out there on the mountain: Abbey and Barclay, Tom, Roderick, Lorimar, and Randolf, and that convinced him to get started pronto.

"All right, then," the Bone said, rolling up his sleeves.

The Rats emerged from the wheelhouse.

"Are we still abandoning ship?" Stinky asked.

"Now why would we want to go and do that?" Percival answered, annoyed.

"The sky ship is ruined," Smelly pointed out. "She will never fly again."

"We'll see about that." Percival marched into the wheelhouse. "Now where did Abbey put my tools?"

Agak's stomach rumbled painfully. The King of the Rats placed clawed hands against the vibrating flesh of his belly, hoping to stifle the sound, but he wasn't the least bit successful.

Agak's soldiers were all staring at him.

"What are you looking at?" he snapped in their Rat Creature tongue.

"We look at someone as hungry as us," said one of the Rat soldiers, as the others nodded in agreement.

"Who said anything about being hungry?" Agak snarled. "The only hunger I feel is for revenge against those imbeciles who stole from me."

The King remembered the two Rats that had crept into his chambers and stole his squirrel. He wished he had that food now.

Agak's stomach protested yet again.

"You do not speak of hunger," the Rat soldier pressed. "But your stomach does."

King Agak surged at them with a roar. "Insolent swine," he growled, fixing them all in an icy stare. "I will be hungry when I am hungry . . . not when you or my stomach tells me so."

He was starving, it was true, as were his soldiers, but he could not lose face, for it was he who had allowed them to be brought to this forsaken place. The King glared at the four humans that were not quite human, and were, for the time being, their allies.

They stood at the base of the vast Pawa Mountains, at the start of a desolate rocky path that would take them to higher elevations. The odd humans stood with their eyes closed, swaying in the cold wind sweeping down off the mountains.

Agak had had enough of them. He only wanted their help in capturing the two Rat fugitives and for the opportunity to feast upon the flesh of a Bone.

The King's mouth began to salivate, drenching the thick, course fur on his chin. He looked to his men, and saw the misery and pain of hunger in their eyes. The inhumans had not allowed them to hunt for food while they pursued the sky ship and its riders.

Agak sniffed the air, searching for a trace of the renegade Rats, but found nothing but the cold scent of mountain stone. The trail had been lost.

The hunger for revenge was great, but his hunger, and the hunger of his soldiers, was growing by the moment. Glancing toward his followers again, the King knew what he would do.

The Rat King approached the inhumans, who stood silently before the mountain trail. Agak cleared his throat with a gurgle, hoping to capture their attention.

"Is there something you want?" the leader of the inhumans asked in the language of the Rat Creatures, not bothering to turn.

"We tire of the chase," Agak spoke with finality. "Our time together is done."

The inhuman leader slowly turned to look at him. Agak felt the fur at the nape of his thick neck prickle as the man's dark, bottomless eyes fell upon him.

"Done?" the leader asked.

Agak nodded with a quick jerk. "We are hungry . . . tired," the Rat King said, averting his eyes. The other inhumans were staring now, too.

"After all we've been through," the leader said.

Agak was silent as he turned his large, shaggy back on them, preparing to join his soldiers.

"The Nacht would have given you everything you desired."

The Rat King stopped. "Nacht?" Agak questioned.

The inhuman leader nodded. "This is where it will all come to a head," he said, pointing up into the fog-enshrouded mountains. "The Nacht has whispered to us that this is where the last stand of the Dreaming's agents will occur."

Agak looked up past the trail and into the thick, shifting haze. "Those who stole from Agak?" he questioned.

The leader nodded. "Those who stole from you, as well as the others . . . including the Bones." The inhuman leader paused. "You've feasted upon a Bone, haven't you?"

The King's stomach painfully churned with digestive juices, his mouth swimming with saliva.

"I thought we already discussed this," he said hesitantly. "No, I haven't."

The inhuman appeared surprised. "Really?" he asked. "You haven't truly tasted meat until you've supped upon the white flesh of a Bone. But that is neither here nor there, for you are leaving our company."

The King stood staring, his gaze going from the inhumans, to his soldiers, and back to the inhumans again.

"Perhaps we will see you again," the leader said, turning with the others of his ilk. "After the Nacht has taken control over all and darkness has spread across the land."

They began to walk the rocky path up into the mountains.

"Wait!" Agak screamed, and they stopped.

The leader slowly faced him. "Yes?"

"Those that we hunt . . ." the Rat King grumbled, pointing a claw up into the shifting gray clouds. "They are up there?"

The leader nodded. "Somewhere, yes. Where the Nacht will be victorious."

"And the Bones?" Agak asked, rivers of spit oozing down his chin to puddle at his clawed feet.

"And the Bones," the leader confirmed with a hint of a smile. "The oh-so-tasty Bones."

King Agak turned to his soldiers.

"Into the mountains!" he proclaimed, a desire burning in his belly the likes of which he had never experienced before.

CHAPTER 5

Randolf stood in front of the home he had abandoned after his family was killed. He couldn't remember how he got there — just that he was, somehow, with his wife and daughter again.

"Why won't you let me in?" he asked as they stood in the doorway, blocking his entrance to their simple home.

Ilana, his wife, stared at him with large, sad eyes. "Because it is not yet your time." She shook her head. "It is not yet *our* time to be together again."

The Veni Yan warrior tried to move closer to them, but an invisible force prevented him from reaching them.

His daughter giggled, hugging her doll as she peered around her mother's waist. "Silly Daddy," Corey said. "You still have very much to do before you come home."

Randolf felt a wave of sadness pass over him. Here in

front of him was all that he had ever wanted, and yet again, it was denied him.

"Please," he said, raising his hands, pressing them against the invisible barrier that kept them apart. "I miss you both so much."

"And we you," Ilana said gently. "But the world still needs you."

"Don't you need me?" he asked, his heart heavy with grief.

"Of course we need you." His wife placed her delicate hands upon their daughter's shoulders. "But the forces of light, the forces of good, right now they need your courage and strength more."

He knew that what she said was true, though the weight of responsibility felt heavy upon his shoulders. As strange as it seemed to him, it appeared that the Valley — and the Dreaming — had need of an old Veni Yan priest who had nearly lost his faith in everything, until a young boy on a mission had shown him his worth again.

Had shown him that he was needed.

Randolf accepted that it was not yet his time to be with his family again. "I will return to you."

"And we'll be waiting," Ilana told him.

Corey ran from her mother's arms, leaned on the barrier that separated them, and kissed it.

"I love you, Daddy," she said, waving good-bye.

The warrior reluctantly stepped away as his family backed into the house to be lost in the darkness behind them. As his home slowly faded away, he promised himself that he would return to them.

When his job was done.

It was raining, or at least that's what Randolf thought as heavy drops spattered onto his face, rousing him from his unconscious state. He looked up to find Abbey Bone's face, her eyes wet with tears.

"You're alive!" the little Bone girl said, suddenly over-joyed.

"I am," Randolf grunted as Abbey threw her tiny arms around his chest and hugged him furiously.

"You're alive, you're alive, you're alive," she cried, voice muffled as she spoke into his chest. "I didn't know what I was gonna do if you were dead."

The Veni Yan patted the little girl's arm as he sat up. "Well, at least there will be no need to worry about that." He looked around, studying their surroundings. They appeared to be on one of the mountain's many cliffs.

Randolf stood and realized he was still wearing the harness that Percival had given him. He looked for the balloon that had carried him off into the sky but saw only its tattered remains.

"We popped it," Abbey said.

Randolf looked at her quizzically. "Excuse me?" he asked as he began to unfasten the harness.

"Your balloon," she said, pointing to the scraps lying on the stony ground. "You were unconscious, and your balloon was still filled with some hot air when we landed, and it was dragging you close to the edge, so we popped it."

"Actually, I bit it," said a squeaky voice from behind Randolf.

The Veni Yan let the harness drop to the ground as he turned to see Roderick climbing down from the rocks.

"I gave it a good nip and then it popped," the raccoon said, jumping down to join them. He was holding something with one of his furry front legs.

"Thank you, Roderick," Randolf said. "It's good to see that we all made it down in one piece."

"We made it down in one piece, but what about the others?" Abbey asked, her young voice trembling with emotion as she struggled to hold back tears. "What about Barclay, Uncle Percy, Tom, and Lorimar?"

Randolf knelt down beside the little Bone. "If we survived, then there is a very good chance that they survived as well."

"Yeah, don't be sad," Roderick added. "I bet even Stinky and Smelly and their stupid dead squirrel survived, too."

"Ya think?" Abbey asked between sniffles.

"Until we know otherwise, we must have faith," Randolf said, rising to his full height.

"No sense in thinking sad thoughts when you don't have to," Roderick said to the little Bone. "And besides, I've got some good news."

"What is it?" Abbey asked, temporarily distracted from her concerns.

Randolf watched as the raccoon removed what he had been carefully holding in the crook of his arm.

"I don't know about you two, but I'm starving," Roderick said, holding out a round, white object in each paw.

"And I found us some eggs."

Tom Elm thought that he might be dead.

He was floating in an ocean of total darkness, and for a moment, he was afraid, until he realized that this darkness was calm . . . peaceful.

Patient.

The boy could sense it as he bobbed there, a sense that something was about to occur.

Something extraordinary.

And suddenly, it happened. There was a blinding flash of warm light — a light like no other — and in that light there was such beauty, wonder, and life. This wonderful light chased away the darkness, replacing it with so much more.

From this light the Dreaming was formed, and all was right.

But the darkness was not a force to be trifled with, for it had existed far longer than the light, and it enjoyed the peace and calm of nothingness. The darkness retreated, resenting the light — resenting the Dreaming — for what had been taken from it.

And from that resentment the Lord of the Locusts was formed.

And the Nacht.

A battle of good versus evil began . . . light against darkness.

Tom continued to float there like some ghostly presence haunting the recollections of the past. Now he knew that this battle had raged since the beginning, that light and dark had always been at odds. And he realized that he'd seen it every day of his young life as dawn chased away the darkness of night, only to have night rule again with dusk.

It was a balance, as it had always been, but the powers of darkness were growing greedy, desiring what they once had.

Before the Spark and the coming of light.

When all was black.

Tom closed his eyes and basked in the warmth of the

light of creation, and for a moment, he was part of it all.

He was one with the light . . . with the Spark.

But then the darkness came again, but not the darkness where evil dwelled. This was like the darkness before.

Calm. Peaceful. Patient.

Waiting.

Tom heard a sound, a calming sound.

Ba-Thump. Ba-Thump. Ba-Thump. Ba-Thump.

He knew that sound, and it brought him great joy. It was the sound of a heartbeat, one that he had not heard since . . .

The light returned, and with it the two people who had given him life and who loved him.

Tom Elm was born, basking in the love of his parents. Feeling the light of life burning inside him.

Tom came awake in a flash. *What does my birth have to do with the Spark?*

"Hey, Tom, you awake?" asked a voice that Tom recognized as Barclay's. Tom tried to get up but found that he couldn't.

"What's going on?" he asked, realizing that both of his wrists and ankles were bound with thick, knotted rope.

"I think it's pretty obvious," Barclay said from somewhere close by. "We're tied up. . . . We've been captured."

Tom was lying on his side and wriggled around on the

hay-covered ground so that he could see the Bone twin leaning against a wooden post.

"There you are. Where are we?"

"Looks like we're in a barn," Barclay replied, nodding toward a pile of hay in the corner and an empty stall where a horse or a cow might have been kept.

Tom heard the sound of feet crunching across rocky ground and could see that someone was moving past the slats of the barn's wall. "Somebody's coming," he warned Barclay.

"Maybe we should pretend to be asleep," the young Bone suggested.

"Good idea," Tom agreed, and they both closed their eyes as the barn door opened with a loud creak and a blast of cold air.

Tom carefully cracked his eyes open and watched a girl enter the barn. She looked to be about his age, with long brown hair, wearing clothes made from tanned animal hide and a hooded cloak around her shoulders. She was carrying a heavy wooden bucket, its contents sloshing around as she walked. It was then that Tom realized how thirsty he was.

"Hello," he said, opening his eyes. "Is that water for us?"

She stopped suddenly, suspiciously studying first him and then Barclay.

"It's all right," Tom said. "We're not going to hurt you or anything."

"Besides, what could we do with our hands and feet tied up?" Barclay chimed in.

The girl said nothing, but carefully moved closer, still far enough away that she could leap back and escape if she had to. She pulled a wooden ladle from the bucket, reached out, and held it close to Tom's lips.

Tom eagerly slurped at the contents, drinking it clean in a matter of moments.

"Could I have some more, please?" he asked. "I'm very thirsty."

"Hey, leave some for me. I'm thirsty, too!" Barclay complained.

She gave Tom some more and then moved to Barclay.

"Can you tell us where we are?" Tom asked her, as Barclay drank from the ladle. "Our sky ship ran into some trouble in the thick clouds surrounding the mountains and we were forced to abandon ship."

The girl did not answer, silently placing the ladle back into the bucket and starting to leave.

"Please," Tom begged.

The girl stopped and looked at him.

"We're not dangerous," he insisted.

But she quickly turned away. "My father, the Chief, has

forbidden me to speak to you," she said in a careful whisper as she headed for the exit.

"Tell your father that we're travelers . . . on a quest. There's something evil in the Valley that we're trying to —"

The girl did not stop to listen, running out as the barn door slammed shut behind her, leaving them alone once more.

"Jeez, she didn't even let you finish," Barclay said.

But Tom could tell that she had heard him, and he hoped that what she heard would get back to her father.

For the sake of them all.

CHAPTER 6

Percival Bone stood inside the ship's hold, assessing the damage to the hull.

"Hmmm, doesn't look too bad," the Bone explorer said to himself. He climbed over the contents of several storage containers that had spilled during the crash and ran his chubby fingers across some of the broken edges of wood in the hull, careful not to get a splinter. The damage didn't appear to be anything that a little reinforcement couldn't fix.

He began to mentally put together a list of things he would need to make the *Queen* airborne again. Finding his toolbox had been easy, but now came the tricky part. As he stood amid the jumbled mess of all that he had been carrying on the ship, Percival wondered how he was ever going to find everything he needed.

Deciding to start by patching the holes in the *Queen*'s body, he rummaged around looking for the extra wood he kept on board for just such an emergency. Carefully, he waded through the debris, not wanting to cause the ship to shift from its resting place and slide down the mountain.

Percival stooped and picked up some folded blankets, tossing them aside. And that's when he heard them — the Rats chattering on the deck above.

Climbing up on an overturned crate, he cupped an ear to the ceiling and listened. He knew that Tom had wanted the ratty pair to be part of the quest — but he still didn't trust the bickering monsters any farther than he could throw them.

"We should leave before the Bone comes back up," one was saying.

"Are you sure it'll be safe?" asked the other. "Remember, it's not just us, we have Fredrick to look after now." Percival knew this one had to be Stinky.

"Will you forget about that stupid dead squirrel for just one moment?" screeched Smelly. "Remember where we are now and who stalks these mountains. We should have left a long time ago."

Percival could not believe his ears. "Why those no-good . . ."

He shifted his footing atop the crate in his agitation,

causing the wooden box to tip to one side. With an angry yelp, Percival fell backward, landing on top of some motor parts and stray potatoes.

He was fighting mad now. He scrambled to his feet and plowed his way through the debris-strewn hold. He had taken those foul-smelling monsters on board his ship against his better judgment, treated them with respect, and this was how they were going to treat him?

He practically flew up the stairs, exploding onto the deck with an accusatory "You!"

"EEEEKKK!" Stinky screamed, jumping into Smelly's hairy arms.

"You two have got some nerve!" Percival stomped across the deck toward the Rat Creatures.

"Nerve?" Smelly repeated, struggling to hold on to his friend. "I don't think we have nerve . . . if we have somehow acquired nerve, it's news to me."

"Don't play dumb with me," Percival scolded. "I heard the two of you — planning on jumping ship when things get a little tough."

"Sneaky, Bone," Stinky said, dropping from his companion's arms. "Listening to our personal conversation, you ought to be ashamed." The Rat was waving the dead squirrel at Percival, pieces of fur falling off the rotting animal and drifting in the wind.

"Don't talk to me about shame." The Bone explorer scowled. "And to think that I almost started to believe I was wrong and you two were actually part of the team . . . guess I was right all along."

Smelly's eyes shrank to slits and the monster Rat snarled, showing off rows of razor-sharp teeth. "Team? We don't need no stinking team," he growled. "We are Rat Creatures, and that's all the team we need. Right, comrade?"

"Actually, I thought it was kinda fun being on a team," Stinky said sadly. "We never got to wear uniforms or anything but —"

"Shut it," Smelly ordered his friend. "Before you embarrass us any more." Smelly turned his angry gaze back to Percival. "We must look after ourselves. We are part of the Rat Creature team, and the Rat Creature team only."

"And the Rat Creature team is very afraid of Rock Jaw," Stinky added, eyes darting about nervously.

Percival was so mad he thought he might burst a blood vessel. He didn't need this nonsense on top of a wrecked sky ship.

"Then what are you still here for?" he asked. "Roque Ja could be here any minute. Go on, get out of here! Who needs you? I certainly don't."

Smelly snarled again. "It's a good thing we're in a hurry," he threatened.

"Or what?" Percival asked, pulling up the sleeves on his coat and clenching his fists.

The Rat quickly turned to his companion. "Come on," Smelly said. "We're leaving." Then he clambered over the side of the ship and down to the rocks below.

"I really did like being on your team," Stinky said as he held up his dead squirrel. "And Fredrick did, too."

And then he was gone, the Rat's huge, furry behind the last thing to go over the side.

"Good riddance!" Percival called after them. He had other, more important things to concern himself with than the likes of them.

He had a sky ship to repair.

The sun had set and it was getting cold in the mountains. Randolf threw some more twigs onto the small fire, hoping they had gathered enough to keep the flames alive and all of them warm for the night. Vegetation was scarce in this rocky region.

"So who wants to eat?" Roderick the raccoon asked, picking up the two bird eggs that he had found. He licked his lips eagerly, waiting for them to answer.

"No, thanks," Abbey Bone said, holding out her hands to the fire.

"You've gotta be hungry," Roderick said. "We haven't had anything to eat since" — the raccoon thought for a moment — "since yesterday," he said, his eyes bulging. "We never had a chance for breakfast with us having to abandon ship and all. You've got to eat something or you'll get sick."

Randolf tossed another small handful of twigs onto the burning pile, feeding the flames. "Roderick is right," the Veni Yan said. "You must eat in order to keep your strength up."

Abbey looked at the eggs and wrinkled her nose. "How are we gonna cook them?" she asked. "We don't have a frying pan or a pot to boil water in."

"You eat 'em like this," Roderick explained. "You open up the top of the shell and eat what's inside."

"Ewwww," Abbey said, turning her head. "No, thank you."

Randolf chuckled. "It's not as bad as you think," he said.

"Then you can have my share," Abbey replied. "I'm not hungry." Randolf knew that keeping up their strength would be very important, seeing as they had no idea how long they would remain in these mountains before — and if — they were somehow reunited with the others.

"Watch me," he said, holding out his hand as Roderick placed one of the eggs in the Veni Yan's palm. Randolf carefully tapped the pointier end of the egg against a rock, then peeled away the broken sections to expose a hole in the egg. "The inside is quite nutritious," he explained.

Abbey continued to look on with disgust as the Veni

Yan brought the egg up, tipping some of what was inside the shell into his mouth.

Randolf swallowed. "See, not so bad."

"Really?" Abbey asked. "Looked kinda gross to me."

"It's not gross," Roderick said, holding out his paws for the egg. Randolf handed it to him. "It's just yolk and stuff." He tipped the egg toward Abbey so she could see inside.

"That looks awful!" she said.

"But it'll keep you strong," he answered before pouring some of the egg's contents into his own mouth. The raccoon chewed a bit, and then swallowed. "Now that's a good bird egg," he said, smacking his raccoon lips.

"You really should try," Randolf said. "You're going to need all your strength if we're to find your brother and uncle, as well as the others." He motioned for Roderick to hand her the egg.

Begrudgingly, Abbey took it, her nose wrinkling all the more as she sniffed it.

"It smells really bad," she said.

"Ignore the smell," Randolf told her. "Imagine that it's your most favorite food."

"Like sponge cake and bratwurst?" she asked.

"Exactly like that," Randolf told her. "Remember how good those things taste . . . remember really hard." He motioned for her to tip the egg into her mouth, and after a moment, she did just that.

Abbey made a face as she drank from the egg, chewing slightly before swallowing with a big gulp.

"No way was that sponge cake *or* bratwurst," she exclaimed with disgust.

"Of course not," Roderick said, taking the egg back from her. "That's because it isn't."

"That was something my wife and I would do to convince our daughter to take her medicine when she was sick," Randolf explained. He grew very quiet, their absence continuing to weigh heavily on him.

"Did it work?" Abbey asked him.

He was so lost in his thoughts of them — of his guilt at having not been there when the Hairy Men attacked — he'd forgotten where he was.

"Excuse me?" the Veni Yan asked.

"Telling your daughter to think of her most favorite food . . . did it get her to take her medicine?"

Randolf held up a single finger. "Once," he said. "It worked once and never again."

They all had a good laugh about that, Roderick finishing off the contents of one egg before moving on to the other. He took a sip of the new egg, then handed it to Randolf, who drank from it.

"This is the first time I've heard about your wife and daughter," Abbey said as she took the egg from him. "Where are they? Are they waiting for you someplace?"

Randolf remembered the dream he'd had. He would have preferred not to have this conversation, but could not ignore the child's question.

"They are no longer with us," the Veni Yan said, feeding the fire with some more of the dried brush and sticks that they had found. "They died many years ago . . . killed by the Rat Creatures while I was away."

Abbey became very quiet, drinking from the egg without any complaint before handing it to Roderick.

"That's very sad," she said.

"It is," Roderick agreed, holding the egg. "The Rats got my parents, too." He took a swig, then handed it off to Randolf again.

"I hope they are waiting for me," Randolf said, having some more of the egg. "Hopefully they will forgive me for not being there to save them."

He offered Abbey the egg again. The little girl shook her head. "No, thank you, I'm done."

Randolf gave the egg back to Roderick.

"You can't blame yourself for not being there," Abbey said to Randolf.

"But I should have been. It was my job to protect them."

"But it was also your job to protect the Valley, right?"

"As a Veni Yan, it was," he answered truthfully.

"Maybe you weren't supposed to be there," she said. "If you were, you might've been killed."

For a very long time, he had wished that he had been, but lately . . .

"And if you were killed, you wouldn't be part of the quest, and you wouldn't be able to help save the Valley . . . and maybe the whole wide world from the Nacht."

It was very quiet around the fire then, the little girl's words far more meaningful than he would have believed possible from a child.

A loud slurping sound disturbed the silence, and they looked over to see Roderick finishing up the contents of the second egg.

"No sense in letting it go to waste," the raccoon said with a toothy smile, and they all laughed.

But the laughter was short lived as there came the sound of something moving through the air. Something moving with great speed.

Something that snatched Abbey Bone up from where she sat with nary a sound.

Up into the night.

Smelly ran across the hard surface, the cold winds whipping down from the highest peaks of the Pawa Mountains and causing his bulbous, round eyes to water. The stink of their mortal enemy, the giant mountain cat, Rock Jaw, was heavy in the air, and it made the Rat Creature's fur bristle with the potential for danger.

"Perhaps we should find a nice cave and wait until morning to continue," the Rat Creature suggested to his friend.

The suggestion got no response, causing Smelly to look over to where he imagined his comrade would be running by his side, but the spot was strangely vacant.

"Stinky?" Smelly called out, gradually having become used to the names given to them by the little — and potentially very tasty — Bone children.

Smelly came to a sudden stop, concerned for his partner's safety. "Stinky, where have you gone?" The Rat Creature turned back to see the sitting shape of his friend way off in the distance.

"What are you doing down there?" Smelly called out. Stinky did not answer, causing Smelly to backtrack. "What's wrong with you?" Smelly asked, berating his friend. "Don't you know the longer we are out in the open like this, the more likely we'll be found by Rock Jaw?"

Stinky sat quietly, petting Fredrick's fur.

"Did you hear me?" Smelly wanted to know.

"Where are we going?" Stinky asked, still petting his dead squirrel.

"Away from here," Smelly answered. "Away from Rock Jaw."

"And then?"

"And then?" Smelly repeated.

"Where will we go after that? We can't go home be-cause King Agak probably still wants us dead. . . . Where will we go?"

"I . . . I . . ." Smelly stammered, unsure of the answer.

"Might as well be on a quest," Stinky said, looking back in the direction where they came from.

"Are you suggesting that we go back?" Smelly asked, not believing his ears.

"At least we had a place to be."

"But . . . but what about Rock Jaw?" Smelly asked, his voice a cautious whisper as he looked around.

"Maybe he won't bother us if we're part of a team," Stinky suggested. "Part of a quest."

Smelly was about to protest, to tell his comrade every-thing that was wrong with his idea, but at that moment, standing on the cold mountainside, he really couldn't come up with anything.

"Do you think Percival Bone will have us back?" Smelly asked.

"Maybe if we ask him nicely," Stinky said.

CHAPTER 7

"So who do you think they are?" Barclay asked.

"I don't really know," Tom answered, trying to get comfortable with his hands tied behind his back.

"Why do you think they tied us up?"

"Don't know that, either. Maybe they don't like strangers."

"That girl said her father was the Chief. . . . That means he's the boss, right?"

"I guess that would be the case." Tom's fingers were getting numb, and he wiggled them around, trying to bring some of their feeling back.

"Where do you think the others are?"

"I don't —"

"Maybe they're out there looking for us right now," the little Bone continued without waiting for an answer.

"That would be nice," Tom said, but he doubted that

was the case. They were in a situation they'd have to deal with on their own.

"So who do you think the guys who captured us are?" Barclay asked again, as if Tom might have come up with the answer in the last thirty seconds.

"I told you, I don't know." Tom was getting annoyed now.

"Pawa . . ." said a tiny, barely distinguishable voice from somewhere in the barn.

"What did you say?" Tom asked.

"I didn't say nothin'," Barclay answered.

"I could have sworn I heard . . ."

"They are the men of Pawa," said the voice again, this time a little louder.

"I know that voice," Tom said, struggling to look around the room. "It's Lorimar! Lorimar, where are you? Hello?"

Tom's eyes searched every dark corner of the barn, but he could not find the source of the voice.

"I'm here," the small voice said.

"Where?" Tom asked.

"Yeah, where are you?" Barclay echoed.

"Here," Lorimar answered. "Down here beneath the straw."

And that was when Tom finally noticed a trace of movement underneath the straw not far from his leg. A slender stalk of brown vegetation rose to attention. Slowly, it began to take on the familiar visage of Lorimar — only far, far smaller.

"Is something wrong with you?" Tom asked as the tiny figure pulled itself from the cold dirt.

"This is a barren region of the Valley," she explained. "Very little vegetation grows here. I've had to make do with one of the only plants that grows here."

"You're so tiny," Barclay announced.

"Thank you for that, Barclay," Lorimar said. "I hadn't noticed."

"So you think it's Pawan people who have us?" Tom asked.

"I do," Lorimar answered. "Which means that we might want to attempt an escape before they can do us any harm." She walked behind Tom to try and loosen his bonds.

"What's wrong with these Pawa people?" Barclay asked nervously. "Are they bad guys or something?"

"They attacked Atheia not too long ago, when the Lord of Locusts was trying to take control," Tom explained. He could feel Lorimar tugging on the knots at his wrists.

"This form is too small," she squeaked.

"If only we had some bacon fat," Barclay said.

"Do I even want to ask?" Tom replied.

"Uncle Percival told Abbey and me about the time he was captured by the Hungraman tribe and how they were going to make him the main course of their feast, but he used bacon fat to slip out of his ropes and escaped."

"Where did he get bacon fat?" Tom was actually curious.

"I don't know," the little Bone answered. "He must've brought some with him."

Tom returned his attention to the plant woman at his back. "Any luck, Lorimar?"

"I'm afraid not. But the boy has given me an idea."

"Bacon fat has given you an idea?" Tom questioned.

Her response was a slight snapping sound, followed by a cool sensation on his wrists.

"What are you doing back there?"

"The plants in this region survive by absorbing and retaining fluids," Lorimar explained. "I've cracked open one of my limbs and let the fluid dribble onto your wrists. See if you can slip free."

"Me next!" Barclay cried out.

While Lorimar helped Barclay, Tom attempted to free his hands. At first he didn't think it was going to work. The plant fluid was a little sticky and slimy, but as he wiggled his wrists around, he could feel the thick rope slowly sliding over his fingers.

"I think it's working!" he exclaimed.

"Do you need me to snap another limb?" Lorimar asked.

"No," Tom said. "I think I've got it. . . ."

There was a cry of excitement from behind him.

"I'm free!" Barclay exclaimed.

And just as the boy announced this, Tom's own hands slipped out from beneath the ropes. He shook the flow of blood back into his hands, then reached down to untie the ropes around his ankles.

He turned to help Barclay with his ropes, but the little Bone slapped his hands away. "I can do it," he protested.

"Well, hurry up," Tom scolded. "We need to get out of here as quick as we can before the Pawan people come back and . . ."

As if on cue, the door to the barn opened, and the girl who had brought them water earlier entered with some men carrying swords and spears.

"Hello," Tom said, not knowing what else to say.

"You're not gonna tie us up again, are you?" Barclay asked.

The girl scowled. "My father wishes to speak with you. I'll leave you untied if you promise to behave yourselves."

"I think we can do that," Tom said, standing.

"Me too," Barclay added.

Randolf reacted with the speed of thought, and maybe faster. He slipped his hand inside his robes to retrieve his dagger and let it fly up into the air — up into the thing that was attempting to steal Abbey Bone away.

There was a scream of pain that chilled him to his soul, but the results were exactly what he had hoped: Abbey was released, dropping to the ground just beyond the fire.

"Roderick, tend to the girl," Randolf, already on the move, ordered. He could hear what had taken the girl struggling to stay aloft, then caught sight of the large, shadowy shape as it fell from the sky to flop upon the rocky ground. He drew the old sword by his side and cautiously approached the thing that was lying in a rounded heap.

"Randolf?" he heard Abbey call out.

"Stay where you are," he said, keeping his eyes on the huddled shape. "Stay with Roderick until I tell you otherwise."

He was close enough now to see that the thing was covered in thick, shiny black fur. He had no idea what it was, but it had stopped moving. His dagger must have killed it.

"Randolf," Abbey called out again. "We don't like being over here all alone."

He was just about to kick the large animal over.

"I'll be back in a . . ."

The thing was still alive.

It turned over with an ear-piercing shriek, and Randolf saw it for what it was. The animal resembled a bat — much larger than it had any right to be — and twisted in such a way that made it more monster than a thing of nature. *Twisted by the evil of the Nacht.* Somehow Randolf knew that.

The bat monster lunged, its huge wings pushing it up off the ground. Randolf tried to drive it back with his sword, but the twisted animal was fast, swatting the blade with one of its wings. As he turned to run, Randolf caught a glimpse of the other wing, which was torn and bloodied. His knife hadn't killed it, but it had rendered it flightless.

Randolf ran, the monster crawling after him with increasing speed. The Veni Yan was about to call to Abbey and Roderick and tell them to hide among the rocks, but there wasn't any need. The pair was suddenly in front of him, having disobeyed his commands to stay at camp.

At first they smiled sheepishly, but their expressions quickly turned to shock and then fright as the evil bat came crawling across the ground with a monstrous shriek.

"Go!" Randolf shouted, waving his arms, but the raccoon and the little girl stood frozen. He didn't slow down as he scooped up Abbey and Roderick, one under each arm.

"Faster, Randolf, faster!" Roderick screamed.

"It's gonna get us!" Abbey shrieked, kicking her feet in panic.

"Stop moving," Randolf ordered, growing tired but refusing to slow down, knowing what their fate would be if he did.

The next thing Randolf knew, he lost his footing and stumbled forward, releasing Abbey and Roderick as he attempted to catch himself. Crashing to his knees, he felt bits of rock and dirt digging into his flesh, but the Veni

Yan didn't have time for pain. He quickly climbed to his feet, shielding where Abbey and Roderick now lay as the monster bat bore down on them.

Weaponless, he prepared to use everything he had ever learned as a warrior to fight the grotesque beast in hand-to-hand combat, but he never got the chance. Something leaped down from a cropping of rock above him before the bat could reach him. Something that pinned the flailing bat to the ground, tearing into its black, hairy flesh with a rumbling growl.

Randolf quickly gathered Abbey and Roderick into his arms and slowly began to back away as the more savage beast continued to rip the bat apart. He hoped that maybe they could get away and find a place to hide before . . .

Sensing their movement, the attacking beast turned its head toward them, its eyes glowing an eerie purple in the moonlight.

"Where do you think you're going?" it asked, its voice like the rumble of an avalanche.

The large animal slowly padded toward them, and they saw it was a large mountain cat . . . a mountain cat that was at least five times the size of an average mountain lion.

Randolf had no doubt that they were now in the presence of the beast called Roque Ja.

Percival had patched the holes in the *Queen*'s hull and had moved on to do the same for the ship's balloons. Night had fallen, but it did little to slow him down. He was sewing on the last of the patches, munching on a stray potato, when he realized that it had been far too many hours since he'd last slept.

The weariness hit him hard, and he was suddenly having a difficult time keeping his eyes open. The Bone stood up, careful not to step on the deflated balloon that he'd worked so hard to fix. Didn't need any more holes, thank you very much.

Percival rubbed his burning eyes and thought about closing them for a quick nap, but then caught sight of the bent and twisted propellers propped up against the ship's side.

There was still much to be done if he wanted to get the *Queen* sky-worthy again.

"All right, then," he said aloud to help rouse himself to action. "Let's get to it."

He popped the last bite of potato into his mouth and eagerly rubbed his hands together while he chewed. His toolbox lay open, but as he reached down to close the lid, he thought he heard something and froze. Head cocked to the side, he listened carefully to the sounds of the nighttime mountains. The wind moaned softly from time to time, but otherwise, things seemed pretty quiet.

Chalking it up to nerves, the Bone closed the cover of his toolbox, latched it, then picked it up and headed for the rope ladder that led up to the *Queen*'s deck. He was just about to take hold of one of the rungs when he heard it again. There was no mistaking it this time — he was no longer alone.

And whatever it was, it was getting closer.

He remembered that the *Queen* had been knocked from the sky by something that lived in these mountains, something with claws sharp enough to tear through the tough fabric of the sky ship's balloons, and decided that it would probably be wise to be ready to protect himself — just in case.

Whistling a cheery tune, he set the toolbox down at the foot of the ladder and bent over, casually unsnapping the lid as if he needed to check for something.

"Now where did I put that . . ."

Percival spun around with a roar, screaming at the top of his lungs, a large metal wrench in his hand.

"Sneak up on me, will ya? I'll show you!"

"YEEEEARRRRRRRRRGGGH!" Stinky and Smelly cried out, the two Rats grabbing hold of each other in sheer terror.

"Oh, it's just you two," Percival said, lowering the wrench. "I thought you'd be long gone by now."

"We . . . we decided to return," Stinky said, trembling, still holding tight to his friend.

"Hrrumph," Percival said. He returned the wrench to the toolbox and slammed the lid closed.

"How selfish would we be to leave you all by yourself in the wreckage of your sky wagon?" added Smelly.

"It's a sky ship," Percival corrected, picking up the toolbox and starting to climb up the rope ladder.

"Aren't you glad to see us?" Stinky asked.

Percival paused. "Oh yeah, I'm just tickled."

The Rats seemed happy about this, missing his sarcasm.

"But if you two want to be part of my crew again . . . part of the team, you're going to have to make yourselves useful."

The pair nodded vigorously.

"Oh yes, we'll be very useful," Stinky said.

"Worth our weight in gizzards," said Smelly.

"Good," Percival said, climbing over the side of the *Queen*. "Either one of you know anything about fixing an engine?"

"What's an engine?" Stinky asked.

Percival shook his head with a sigh.

It was going to be a long night.

CHAPTER 8

Night was almost over, and there had been no attack from the black, nameless things that swooped down upon their village.

Chief Gnod sat in his chair deep in thought. He wondered if his prisoners, those who had floated from the sky, had anything to do with the misfortunes that had been heaped upon his people of late.

"Where are they?" Gnod grumbled, moving uneasily in his seat. The lack of sleep was not doing much for his patience or his disposition.

His wife sat in a chair close by. "She hasn't been gone that long, Gnod," she scolded. "Give the girl a chance."

His daughter, Gerta, had accompanied his men to the barn where the prisoners were being kept. He had not wanted her to become involved in any way, but telling her this . . . it was like talking into a raging wind. It did no good; she did what she wanted to do.

Gnod was about to order another of his tribe out to see what was taking them so long, when the large wooden door to the hall creaked open.

Gerta was the first to enter, followed by the two prisoners — the boy and the Bone child — and the Chief's four soldiers.

The Chief squinted through bleary, sleep-deprived eyes as the procession approached. "Gerta, why are the prisoners not bound?" he bellowed, his powerful voice echoing about the wooden structure.

"They mean us no harm," Gerta answered. "Tom and Barclay have given their word that —"

"Their word!" Gnod rose from his seat, gripping the hilt of the sword he wore at his side.

"Father, please," Gerta begged, as the boy prisoner moved around her and headed straight for the Chief.

Gnod pulled his sword just as the boy stopped and dropped to his knees.

"Chief," he began, holding his hands out, palms up. "Your daughter speaks the truth. We mean you and your people no harm."

The little Bone joined the boy, also falling to his knees. "I don't, either," he said.

The four soldiers moved to surround the youths, weapons ready, as Gerta looked on with displeasure.

"And why should I trust the likes of you?" Gnod asked, still pointing his blade at them.

Tom looked up, and his eyes met the Chief's.

"Why not?" he asked.

The Chief hesitated for a moment, then returned his sword to its sheath and sat heavily in his chair.

"I know nothing of you and your little friend here, other than that you fell out of the sky and onto my mountain." He eyed them suspiciously.

"What do you want to know?" Tom asked. "Ask me anything."

"You can ask me stuff, too," the Bone added.

Gnod stroked his long, graying beard as he considered their offer.

"Why are you here?" he asked.

"We're actually here by accident," Tom began to explain. "Our sky ship got hit with some pretty nasty winds and —"

"Sky ship?" Gnod asked incredulously. "Are you magic users?"

"No, not at all," Tom said. "Barclay's uncle is a great explorer and inventor, and he has this ship that sails through the air. . . ."

"And it uses potatoes for power," Barclay added.

"Yeah," Tom agreed. "And it floats by hanging from these three things called balloons that are filled with gas and —"

"You mock me," the Chief yelled, leaning forward in his chair. "It is not wise to mock a Pawa Chief."

"Oh no, we're not mocking you at all, sir," Tom said quickly.

"Nope, no mocking here," Barclay agreed, shaking his head. "Wouldn't be doing that."

"We really did come on a sky ship, but it was damaged by something that attacked us from the mountains, and we were forced to abandon ship."

"The ship that sails through the air?" the Chief asked.

"That's right," Tom said. "So we had to jump off the ship, wearing smaller balloons that allowed us to float down safely."

Gnod remembered that they had found the boy and his friend wearing strange belts and the floating bubbles of cloth. "This . . . balloon," he said, "this is what let you drop from the sky?"

"We floated," Barclay answered. The Bone held up one of his hands and brought it down slowly.

The Chief leaned back in his chair, digesting what he was hearing. He knew that these two were special, but the information they gave him was nearly beyond comprehension.

"How do I know you're not spies?" Gnod accused. "Spies from Atheia, eager for revenge against us for our part in joining with the Hooded One and attempting to invade your kingdom."

Tom shook his head. "We're not spies. Barclay and I are on a quest."

"A quest?" the Chief inquired. "What kind of quest?"

"A terrible darkness is spreading," Tom said, his young features growing very still and serious. "A threat to Atheia . . . to your tribe . . . to the whole Valley."

The boy rose to his feet, his chest swelling proudly. "And we have been given the task to stop it."

Somehow Gnod could sense that the boy was speaking the truth. He himself had felt it in the air, riding heavily upon the wind. *Maybe that is what we've been experiencing?* he considered. *Maybe we aren't being punished for my foolishness.*

Gnod stared at the boy standing before him and was almost driven to laughter. A mere boy given the task of stopping an evil spreading across the land? It was madness. The boy was telling a fantasy . . . telling lies about his ship that sailed the skies and an infecting darkness.

"I've heard enough," the Chief said wearily. "Take them back to the barn and restrain them," he ordered.

"Father?" Gerta asked. "Why are you . . ."

"Please, Chief," Tom begged, struggling as the soldiers took hold of his arms. "You have to believe me!" he cried as they dragged him from the hall. "If we don't stop the Nacht . . ."

"The Nacht?" the Chief asked. "What's that, boy? Another of your fantasies?" He waved them away.

"He's telling the truth!" Barclay shouted from beneath the arm of a soldier who had picked him up.

"I'm too old for fairy stories," the Chief said. "I'll decide the prisoners' fates come noontime, once I've had a chance to sleep."

Gerta strode toward him angrily. "I think you should listen to them," she said.

The Chief looked to his wife. "Take her home," he ordered. "I'm too tired to deal with any more nonsense and —"

The door into the hall flew open, and an old woman rushed in with a cold look of terror on her aged face.

"Chief Gnod! They've come!" she screeched. "The shadow beasts have come again!" She dropped to the ground in a trembling heap.

Chief Gnod felt as though he'd been struck by lightning and leaped up as the sounds of screams wafted into the great hall.

His soldiers waited for him to give them an order, but

the Chief saw the look in their eyes. They had no desire to go out and share the fate of all the others who had been taken over the long, dark nights.

Gnod cringed at the muffled sounds of flapping wings and the cries that started strong and then dwindled as his people were carried off. He dared not look in his daughter's eyes, for he was certain that he would see a reflection of what he felt about himself.

Disappointment.

The boy named Tom shrugged off the hands of the soldiers and strode toward him. "Let me go out there," the boy said. The Chief could see that the boy was afraid as well, but the fear did not incapacitate him — it spurred him to action. "I think I can help. . . . Let me go out there."

Chief Gnod hesitated, the screaming outside going on and on.

"What do you have to think about?" the boy cried. "If something happens to me, you don't have to worry about what to do with me anymore."

"Go," the Chief finally said.

Tom carefully opened the door, and the cries got louder.

"Wait for me!" the young Bone said, following his friend into danger.

The Chief was about to order the door barricaded, when he saw Gerta rushing after them.

"Gerta!" he cried out. "You come back here at once!"

She stopped momentarily, turning to face him with an angry glare that was like a physical blow in its intensity.

"You can't," Gnod managed.

"Watch me," she said, pushing his soldiers out of the way and rushing after the boy and the Bone into the fearsome night.

It was early morning, and the sun should have started its ascent into the sky, but it was still dark in the silent village.

As black as night.

"It's so quiet," Porter said as they traveled along the path that led through the normally bustling village.

Stillman looked around, his Dragon eyes observing every pocket of darkness, every shadow. Something was very wrong.

"Shouldn't there be some activity here?" the old turtle asked. "Somebody up and around, getting a start on the day?"

They passed a baker's shop and saw a man lying face-down in the street, loaves of bread scattered around him.

Porter crept from the shadows of the road, moving closer. "What's happened to him?" the turtle asked.

"He's asleep," the Dragon answered, his eyes finding even more villagers who had fallen down where they stood.

"But why is he out here? If he was going to sleep, shouldn't he be in his bed?" Porter asked.

"I don't think he had a choice," Stillman said, looking

around. "I don't think any of them did."

The turtle stood above the sleeping man, poking him repeatedly with a claw.

"You mean there's more?" Porter asked, extending his neck from his shell to peer into the darkness of the village.

"Yeah," Stillman said, the sensation of dread he had been feeling since hitting the road with his friend deepening. This was what the Red Dragon had been talking about. This was what the Dreaming wanted him to help stop. "I think the whole village is like this."

"What's happened to them?" Porter wanted to know. "Why are they all asleep?"

Stillman listened carefully. He could hear the sounds of fitful slumber, moans and cries, drifting on the early-morning breeze.

"Something has made them this way," the Dragon said. "Something that we have to try and stop."

"Us? Stop this?" The turtle looked around again. "I don't know about that," he said nervously. "It all seems so big and scary."

"It does, doesn't it?" Stillman agreed. "But the Dreaming and the Red Dragon picked us for this special job for a reason."

"Maybe because nobody else was stupid enough to take it," Porter said, growing more afraid.

"Or we're just that special," Stillman said, trying to instill some confidence in his friend, as well as shore up his own. "So special that nobody else could possibly pull it off except us."

"I don't know," the little turtle said. "This looks an awful lot bigger than what a turtle and a Dragon can handle."

"You'd be surprised what a couple of guys like us can accomplish," Stillman said, stamping down his fear. The Dreaming and Red Dragon were depending on him, and he had no intention of disappointing them. And besides, there was way too much at stake.

He turned his face upward and breathed another plume of special fire up into the air. They both watched as the orange fire again took the shape of an arrow, pointing them onward.

"We better keep moving," the Dragon said.

The Nacht was excited; everything was going splendidly, and very soon he would no longer have the Dreaming and her silly little followers around to interfere with his grand designs.

The great Dragon of shadow waded among those taken in their sleep — a vast ocean of bodies of every conceivable size and shape held firmly in the grip of nightmare. He admired his collection, experiencing another twinge of excitement at the prospect of its growth.

The Dreaming had served him well, her weakness allowing him the ability to reach out to those unaware of his existence and to pluck them from the Waking World and into the world of shadow.

"Where is your power now?" he asked the sleeping Dragons, the Veni Yan dream masters, the queens, and the peasants. "Your Dreaming tries to stop my march but . . ."

The air was suddenly filled with spirits, ghostly creatures that served the Nacht.

"What is the Dreaming doing now?" asked one of the spectral beings.

"Has she given up all hope of defeating you?" asked another.

"Or does she still fight, never giving in until the battle is won?" added a third.

The great black Dragon spread its wings of ebony shadow, rearing back as he roared. "Silence!" bellowed the Nacht. Clouds of black plumed from his open mouth as the evil spirits darted away to escape the Dragon's wrath. "Yes, the Dreaming fights on," the Nacht said. "Too stubborn to realize that her efforts are in vain."

The Dragon strolled across the land that was once the Dreaming, its thick, luscious jungles now choked with shadow. The Nacht swished his powerful tail, sending clouds of billowing darkness into an atmosphere already choked with soot.

The spirits followed, eager to hear their master's words.

"The Dreaming's servants have been separated. They have been divided and therefore are ineffectual."

"Like the Spark," said one of the spirits.

"Yes," agreed the Nacht. "No threat to me now that they are no longer together."

"But the Spark . . . is it not nearly whole again?" questioned another of the ghostly entities.

"It is," said the Nacht, coming to stop at what looked to be a great wall.

A wall of solid darkness.

The wall that separated the land of the Dreaming from the Waking World.

"As soon as it is whole, it will be given to me," the Dragon said. He reached up with a hooked claw and probed the wall, as if searching for a weakness. "A traitor in their midst will see to that."

The Nacht continued to touch the wall, rearing back upon his thick legs, feeling the vibrations . . . the life that existed on the other side.

"And when the Spark is in my possession, the barriers will at last come down."

The spirits flew around the Nacht's head.

"And what then, great Dragon of shadow? What then?"

"Then? Then there will be a monstrous flood of darkness into the Waking World, and it will be mine.

"The light of life will shine no more."

CHAPTER 9

Percival wiped beads of sweat from his brow as he stepped back from the *Queen*'s engine. It had been banged up pretty good in the crash, but it was nothing he couldn't handle. Realign some gears, grease up a few cogs, and replace a belt or two, and she would be as good as she was before they'd been brought down. The Bone explorer shivered with the memory, but at least they'd managed to survive.

Well, he and the Rats had.

He thought of the twins again. This was exactly what he'd been afraid of and why he'd never wanted to bring them on his adventures.

Percival closed the door on the engine box and clipped it shut. He would only think of getting the *Queen* back into the sky for now. Then he'd worry about finding Abbey and Barclay, as well as his new friends.

He crossed the deck and peered over the side to see how

his helpers were doing. The Rats were right below him, working on straightening out one of the bent propellers. Smelly laid the propeller on the flat side of a portable anvil, while Stinky attempted to pound the bend out of it. They didn't seem to be doing that badly, considering they hadn't even known how to hold a hammer before getting started.

"How's it going, guys?" Percival called down.

Distracted, Stinky brought the hammer down on Smelly's fingers.

"YEOOWCH!" the Rat screeched, pulling back his hand and doing a crazy dance.

"I told you to be careful," Stinky scolded.

"Me be careful?" Smelly objected, blowing on his clawed fingers. "It is you who should be more careful. I knew you'd be a menace with that hammer."

"Oh, and I suppose you could do better?" Stinky asked.

"I certainly could," Smelly replied with a snarl, snatching the heavy tool from his comrade's claws.

With a sigh, Percival climbed over the side of the *Queen*. "That'll be enough of that," he said, taking the hammer from Smelly's grasp.

"But I was about to show him how good I could be with a hammer," the Rat protested.

"I know exactly what you were about to do. And we don't have time for that kind of nonsense right now."

Stinky had turned his back on them, talking to his

flea-bitten dead squirrel again. "Nobody understands," he was saying. "I try to do my best, and this is what I get for it."

Percival hooked the hammer through the loop of his belt and reached for the propeller blade. "This actually looks great."

Smelly and Stinky were suddenly paying attention again.

"You two did really good work here," the Bone added.

"I did?" Stinky asked, surprised. "Of course I did. . . . See?" he added, glaring at his companion.

"Well, I did good work, too," Smelly added. "And I have the injuries to show for it." He held up swollen fingers.

"Let's get this propeller attached again and then see what we can do about inflating these balloons," Percival said quickly.

That seemed to calm the Rats' hostility, and together they attached the propeller and then spread out the balloons. Percival went to the wheelhouse and stared down at the control panel. If he'd done his job, the ship's engine would turn over, and hot gas would fill the balloons.

"Are we ready, guys?" he called, sticking his head out from the wheelhouse.

The Rats were standing around the deflated balloons.

"What if this doesn't work?" Stinky asked nervously.

"Why must you be so negative?" Smelly scolded. "We must remain positive. Of course it will work."

"But what if it doesn't?" Stinky continued.

Smelly stared at the balloons spread out on the deck. "Then Rock Jaw will probably find us and eat us."

"Thank you, Mr. Positive," Stinky said, looking even more panicked.

"Here goes nothing," Percival said. He flipped the switch and held his breath . . . as the engine roared to life.

He left the wheelhouse to stand with the Rats, and they all stared at the balloons. Little by little they saw movement in the silky material as the balloons gradually started to fill.

They cheered, whooping and hollering and excitedly jumping into one another's arms. Then, suddenly realizing what they were doing, the three jumped back, putting an end to the temporary insanity brought on by their jubilance.

"Looks like we did good," Percival said, crossing his arms.

"We did, didn't we?" Smelly agreed.

"I think I'm going to cry," Stinky said as he wiped his face with the tattered remains of his squirrel.

The Veni Yan priest and the great mountain cat stared at each other for what seemed like hours, each waiting to see what the other might do. Randolf stood in front of Abbey and Roderick but could feel them peering around him.

The cat crouched, his large yellow eyes following the movement.

"Are you the one called Roque Ja?" Randolf asked.

"Perhaps," the animal growled.

Randolf felt a tug at his britches and glanced down to see Roderick attempting to get his attention.

"That's Rock Jaw for sure," the raccoon whispered, pronouncing the name as the Rat Creatures had. "I've met him before." The raccoon stepped out into the open. "Hi, Rock Jaw," he said cheerily. "It's Roderick. Remember me?"

"No," the cat said gruffly, his large eyes squinting as he watched the tiny animal hungrily.

Roderick darted back behind the Veni Yan. "Oh, sorry," he nervously apologized. "Must've got you mixed up with some other huge cat."

"I would like to thank you for coming to our assistance," Randolf said with a polite bow.

Roque Ja casually looked about his surroundings. "I did no such thing," he said. "I was hunting for something tasty." A strange look suddenly came over his large face and he emitted a horrible, throaty gurgling sound before spitting up the chewed and ragged remains of the monstrous bat that he'd eaten.

"That was not tasty," Roque Ja said, pawing at the spit-covered remnants of the bat. He turned his attention back to the group. "Are you tasty?"

Randolf tensed. "I doubt that we would be worth the effort," the Veni Yan said as he reached within the folds of his clothes for his knife . . . that wasn't there. He'd forgotten that he'd thrown it at the evil bat, and his sword wasn't handy, either. Already his brain raced with alternatives for how he would protect Abbey and Roderick, as well as himself, if the cat should pounce.

Roque Ja continued to stare hungrily, the tension between them mounting, when Abbey decided to defuse the situation.

"You don't want to eat us," the little Bone girl said, coming out from hiding.

"Abbey, no!" Roderick warned, but she ignored him.

Randolf reached for her, but the child eluded his grasp. He expected Roque Ja to pounce on such easy prey, but the great cat simply studied the child.

"Are you a Bone?" the beast asked.

"I'm Abbey Bone," she answered. "And you're Roque Ja, right?"

"Why are you in *my* mountains, Bone?" the cat asked. "The last time there were Bones in my mountains . . . let's just say things were troublesome."

"We were looking for you," Abbey told the cat.

"Looking for me?" Roque Ja asked.

"Uh-huh." The little Bone nodded vigorously. "You see, we're on a quest — me, my brother, my uncle Per-

cival, this kid named Tom, Randolf and Roderick here" —
she hooked a thumb toward them — "a plant lady named
Lorimar, and two stupid Rat Creatures."

"Rat Creatures?" the mountain cat repeated with a snarl
that showed off large, pointed white teeth.

"Yep," she said. "And we're all looking for the last pieces of something called the Spark, which is supposed to be
able to stop this really creepy thing called the Nacht."

Roque Ja stared with little emotion before responding.
"And what does this have to do with me?" he asked.

"You're supposed to help us," she said. "You're supposed
to be a part of our quest."

"I'll do no such thing," the cat growled.

"If you don't help, the Nacht is going to do really horrible things to your mountains, the Valley, and maybe even
the whole wide world."

"The evil is already spreading," Randolf continued.
"The sun is shrouded in the sky and there's this twisted
mockery of life." He pointed to what was left of the evil
bat. "It's already begun."

Roque Ja seemed to consider this. "Perhaps that would
explain what is happening down in those caves," the cat
said, a large paw on his chin.

The statement piqued the Veni Yan's attention. "What
do you mean?"

Roque Ja glared at him, then quickly looked away, ignoring his question. "Perhaps I need to investigate this further." He turned, and, as if they weren't even there, strolled away, his large tail swishing behind him.

Randolf, Abbey, and Roderick slowly started to follow until the giant cat stopped abruptly.

"I recommend that you not follow me," Roque Ja snarled without turning.

"So what're we going to do?" Roderick asked Randolf and Abbey.

"What do you think?" Abbey asked, watching the great mountain cat go.

"We follow him," Randolf answered, darting over to retrieve his knife and sword from where they lay.

And the three did just that.

Tom charged from the hall. He wasn't sure what he would see or even what he would do once he saw it.

But he knew that he had to do something.

"What's going on, Tom?" Barclay asked, racing along beside him.

The village was in chaos, women and children running and waving their hands about their heads, but Tom still couldn't see the cause of their panic.

Until something dropped from the murky sky. It swooped down on a mother and child, knocking them both to the ground. The mother fought bravely, but the thing of darkness was stronger, shrieking shrilly as it swatted the woman aside with a black, leathery wing before snatching up the wailing little boy in its talons and flying off.

"No!" Tom cried, unsure of what to do.

"What are they, Tom?" Barclay asked, as more of the creatures dove out of the roiling clouds above the village.

"I . . . I don't know," Tom said.

"They were once simple creatures," squeaked a tiny voice. Tom glanced down to see the miniature Lorimar poking out from one of his pockets. "But now they've been twisted by the power of the Nacht."

"I wondered where you'd gone," Tom said. "What can we do against those . . . things?" he asked, watching the large batlike monsters filling the skies above the village.

"Fight them to the best of your ability," Lorimar said. "That's all that can be asked of you."

"It's not much," Tom said, running toward a cart filled with hay while keeping his eyes on the flying beasts. "But it'll have to do."

They resembled the bats he would often see flying around his home at night, hunting for bugs to eat. But these things were far larger and had been transformed into monsters.

And seemed to be very intent on carrying off as many of the villagers as they could.

Tom pulled a pitchfork from the hay cart, stopping to

look at the sharp prongs. *This should do some damage*, he thought.

"You stay here," he told Barclay, who was crouched down alongside the cart, terrified.

"But I want to help," the little boy said.

"Help me by staying here, all right?" Tom asked.

Barclay nodded, and Tom charged ahead, pitchfork at the ready.

A little boy emerged from a house of wood and thatch, eyes wide with fear as he watched the black bats dart and weave in the sky. Tom was about to yell to the child to get back inside, when the little boy panicked. He screamed as he ran from the safety of the structure and out into the open.

The movement caught the awful red eyes of one of the bat beasts, and it flew at the unsuspecting youth.

The thing drove the screaming child to the ground, sinking its talons into the little boy's shoulders and starting to haul him up into the dingy sky.

"Put him down!" Tom yelled, sticking the pitchfork's sharp prongs into the bat's belly. The abomination shrieked in pain and dropped the child. Tom went to the crying boy, but the bat had not yet given up. It launched itself at Tom, driving him back to the ground.

The pitchfork was knocked from his hands, and Tom threw up his arms as the bat fell upon him. The beast was heavy, its large wings like wet blankets, slapping the ground eagerly as it beared down on him. Tom put his hands around its throat, keeping its snapping jaws from his face.

But for how long?

The monster was strong, far stronger than a twelve-year-old boy, and he could already feel his arms weakening, trembling with exertion as the beast strained to get at him.

The bat was winning, and Tom thrashed from side to side, hoping to roll his infernal attacker from him, but in the struggle something else occurred.

As Tom fought with the bat, his shirt had opened, revealing the nearly completed piece of the Spark that he wore about his neck. The Spark flared to life, bathing the hideous thing in its warm brilliance.

The bat cried out in agony, flipping backward off the boy, allowing Tom to scramble across the ground and get to his feet.

Just then, another monster dropped down in front of him, fangs bared. Tom grabbed the glowing stone at his throat, holding it up to repel the bat, but the beast had something for him, too — it spit a wad of black gunk from its disgusting mouth. The stinking, black substance struck Tom's chest, covering the Spark's searing glow.

Tom tried to brush the tarlike material from the stone

to little avail, as the bat came at him with a hiss. Stumbling back, the heel of his shoe caught on the bat that had been burned by the light of the Spark, and Tom went down on his butt, staring up at the nightmarish sight of the monster gliding toward him.

What happened next was completely unexpected. The pitchfork that he'd used earlier was rammed into the monster's side, and it cried out in pain.

Tom was shocked to see Barclay and the Chief's daughter driving his winged attacker to the ground and pinning it there.

"You all right, Tom?" Barclay asked, out of breath.

"Looked as though you could use some help," Gerta said, a slight smile playing at the corners of her mouth.

Tom knew that it wasn't really time to notice something like this, but she was really pretty. He couldn't stop looking at her chestnut hair, the flush of apple red on her pale cheeks, and her eyes.

She had amazing eyes.

And they were suddenly opened wide and filled with fear.

Two more of the bat monsters had descended, their talons gripping the girl's shoulders, and had started to carry her off.

"No!" Tom screamed, running toward them.

Barclay was closest, and the little Bone grabbed hold of the girl's ankle, trying to pull her back down to the ground. But the combined power of the two bats was too much, and they dragged her up into the sky, Barclay still holding on to her foot.

Tom moved as quickly as he could, pulling the pitchfork from the dead bat, but he was too late. He watched as the pretty girl who had saved his life and Barclay Bone became smaller and smaller until they were specks in the twilight sky.

And then they were gone.

CHAPTER 10

The evil spirit leader looked out through the Constable's eyes as he climbed up into the mountains. He could feel his master's presence in the air around them and in the jagged rocks. He was growing stronger by the minute.

Drawing them up.

The other spirits possessing the bodies of deputies could feel it as well. The world was on the cusp of change, and the possessed Constable and his followers hoped that they would be part of the awesome transformation.

"How much farther?" one of his deputies whined over the howling winds that threatened to rip them from the rocky mountain face.

"As far as it needs to be," the Constable snapped.

He knew that the Nacht was not pleased with their performance so far. They had been placed in the Waking World to stop the agents of the Dreaming, but they'd had little luck — even with the addition of the filthy Rat Creature beasts.

The Constable gazed below him to see the Rat King, Agak, and his own soldiers also scaling the mountain. He was amazed at what the promise of a little Bone flesh could do.

But then again, he and the other spirits were motivated by the idea of permanently inhabiting the human bodies that they now possessed. They had grown fond of them and hoped they would be allowed to keep them if they could get back in their dark lord's good graces.

This is what urged them on, up into the inhospitable mountains. But they would need to show the Nacht that they were worthy of this prize by fulfilling what they had been sent there to do.

And they would finally bask in the shadow of his praise.

Roque Ja walked ahead of them.

Randolf was certain that the big cat knew they were there, even slowing down from time to time when they lagged behind, but he never directly addressed them.

Randolf watched as the great cat gracefully hopped up onto a ledge and disappeared from view. Roderick quickly scampered up the rocks to have a look around. "Hey, guys, you're gonna want to see this."

Randolf lifted Abbey as high as he could so that the little Bone could get her footing and climb the remainder of the way on her own. The Veni Yan followed, joining the two as they stood outside the entrance of a great cave.

"It appears that Roque Ja might have come home," Randolf said. Just inside the entrance, they could see random bones of animals picked clean of their meat.

"Maybe I'll wait out here," Roderick said with a gulp.

"None of those bones belong to anybody we know . . . do they?" Abbey asked, afraid to look too closely.

"No," Randolf consoled, placing a comforting hand on her shoulder. "These are animal bones," he said. "And they appear to have been here for quite some time."

Carefully he moved toward the entrance. "Behind me, now," Randolf instructed as they moved into the cave.

"I thought I told you not to follow me," Roque Ja grumbled as he suddenly loomed out of the darkness before them.

"AHHHHHH!" both Abbey and Roderick cried, each of them taking hold of one of Randolf's legs in a death grip.

"We weren't following you," Randolf said emphatically. "This just so happens to be where we were going as well."

Roque Ja studied him, his yellow eyes glowing eerily in the murk, before the great cat turned and sauntered farther into the cave.

"I thought for sure we were goners," Roderick said, releasing Randolf's leg.

"Me too," Abbey agreed. "For a minute, I thought we were gonna be more bones on the floor."

Randolf started to follow the cat. "If he was going to eat us, he would have done it by now," the Veni Yan said. "I believe he wants us here."

They all moved through the cave behind Roque Ja, careful not to step on the animal skulls, rib cages, and stray bones that littered the floor.

"Somebody needs to do some serious cleaning," Abbey commented as they passed from the main chamber of the cave into another at the far back of the cat's den. They found Roque Ja lying down in front of a large section of wall, licking at one of his large paws.

Randolf noticed an extremely large crack extending from the floor and up across the expanse of wall like a jagged bolt of lightning.

"Is this what brought you here?" the cat asked them.

"Perhaps," Randolf said, drawn to the jagged opening.

"It was never here before," Roque Ja said. "It appeared a few days ago, when the dark clouds first began to cover the sun."

There was a strange greenish glow emanating from inside the crack, and Randolf peered inside. A thick, luminescent moss clung to sections of the wall, illuminating a twisting path into the heart of the mountain.

"Where does it lead to?" Roderick asked, his voice filled with awe.

"Someplace I don't think I want to go," Abbey answered, peeking into the crack.

Roque Ja rose and strolled over to the opening. "Really, little Bone?" the great cat questioned, sticking his nose into the crack and sniffing at the moist air. "I would gather that this is exactly where you need to be."

"Why's that?" Abbey questioned.

"What's to be found inside, Roque Ja?" Randolf asked.

"Strangeness," the cat said, climbing through the large crack and into the cavern beyond. "Things that I did not understand until I came across the likes of you, with your stories of a quest and evil that could change my world."

"They're more than stories, I'm afraid," Randolf said.

"Yes," the cat said, pausing momentarily to study them. "I believe they are."

Roque Ja continued on, eerie shadows being thrown by the light of the glowing lichen. "Are you coming or not?"

And although his instincts screamed of danger, Randolf knew that there was no choice but to follow.

To follow the path laid out for them by the Dreaming.

Porter was tired. He and Stillman sat at the base of the burgeoning mountain range, warming themselves by a dwindling fire.

The Dragon grabbed some more twigs and broken branches from a tiny pile they had gathered and tossed them into the dying flames. He then cleared his throat and gave the fire a little help with a blast of his fiery Dragon's breath.

"Thanks," Porter said, holding his limbs out to the crackling warmth. "It's a lot colder out here than I thought it would be. Remember, I'm usually hibernating now."

"I know," Stillman said, staring into the fire. "And I really do appreciate you coming with me. I don't know if I could do this alone."

"That's all right," Porter said, reaching down to rub

warmth into his turtle feet. "It's the least I could do after you protected us for so long."

Stillman thought about all those years in the forest and the friends who he'd seen come and go. It had been a good life as a forest protector, but he had a sense now that it had all been leading to this.

"And now I've got to protect everyone in the Valley," the little Dragon said.

Porter nodded, mesmerized by the dancing flames. "So what did the Red Dragon tell you exactly, anyway?" he finally asked.

"He really didn't go into specifics, but he said that I was going to be needed for something special," Stillman explained. "That I'm here and not with the other Dragons for a reason . . . for a very special purpose."

"More special than forest protector?" Porter asked.

"I guess this is even bigger than that."

"Wow," Porter said. "How does that make you feel?"

"Important," the little Dragon said, "but a little nervous, too."

"What are you going to have to do?"

"All I know is that I have to help stop something very bad from happening," Stillman said. "That my flame is pretty special and will take me where I need to be."

"Do you know what you're gonna half'ta do?" Porter asked him.

"Not yet," the little Dragon said. "But the Red Dragon said I'd know when it was time."

The pair sat silently for a moment, staring into the warming fire.

"I think I'm pretty rested," the little turtle said, looking to his friend.

"Are you sure?" Stillman asked. "We could probably hold off for a little while longer."

"No," Porter said with a shake of his head. "The sooner we get this done, the sooner everybody in the Valley is safe."

"Good point," the little Dragon said as he leaned back his head and breathed a plume of fire into the air. It again took the shape of an arrow and pointed them through some sparse trees and to the mountains beyond.

"Guess we're going to have to climb," Porter said unenthusiastically.

"Looks that way," Stillman said.

"Are you scared?" Porter asked.

Stillman thought a bit before he answered. "A little," he said. "I'm scared that maybe I won't do a good job . . . that I'll fail."

"Well, you were a really good forest protector," Porter assured him.

"Thanks, buddy," the Dragon said, reaching over and patting his friend's shell. "It's things like that, and the fact that the Red Dragon picked me and not any other Dragon, that makes me think maybe I *can* do this."

"Well, I think you can," Porter agreed. "And I don't even know what you're gonna be doing."

The little Dragon stared at his friend, his Dragon face twisting up in a pleasant smile.

"What's that for?" Porter asked him.

"I think I finally figured out why the Red Dragon wanted me to bring you along on this mission."

Porter smiled back, then stood and stretched his stubby arms over his head. "We should go."

Stillman stood up, too. "You're probably right." He leaned into the dwindling fire and took a deep breath, sucking the fire back into his lungs, leaving behind only the smoldering sticks and twigs.

"That's that," the Dragon said, patting his belly. He turned to the fluttering arrow of flame. It slowly floated up the mountain path, so they began to climb after it.

"Just let me know when you get too tired or cold," Stillman said to Porter. He grabbed hold of an outcropping of rock and pulled himself up, then realized that his friend hadn't replied. He turned and looked below to see that the turtle was having some difficulty getting started.

Stillman climbed back down to his friend.

"Sorry, Stillman," Porter said sadly. "I'm really not built for climbing."

The Dragon reached over to give his friend's round head an affectionate rub. "That's all right," he said, turning his back to Porter. "Hop on and I'll climb for both of us."

"Are you sure?" Porter asked.

"Well, you don't expect me to make this part of the journey without you, do ya?" Stillman asked.

"No, I guess not."

"Then you better come aboard," Stillman said, leaning down so that the little turtle could get onto his back.

And they began to climb.

CHAPTER 11

Tom was paralyzed.

"What do I do?" he asked, staring at the spot in the sky where the bat monsters had just flown off with Barclay and the girl.

The small, spindly form of Lorimar pushed from his pocket and dropped to the rocky ground. "Remain calm, Tom," she said in her small whisper of a voice.

"I can't remain calm," he retorted. "Those . . . those *things* took Barclay and the Chief's daughter. I have to do something."

"You must concern yourself with what is most important to the quest," Lorimar said.

"The quest?" Tom repeated, not believing his ears. "Who can think of the quest now?"

"You should," the plant woman scolded. "Look about

you, Tom Elm, the power of the Nacht is growing, already affecting the Waking World. Are two lives more important than all the lives in the Valley and the world beyond?"

"I can't think of it that way," Tom said. "I have to do something. . . . I have to save them!"

The people of the village wandered around him in shock, and he listened to the cries of those who had lost loved ones to the flying beasts.

"We have to do something," Tom said, trying to get their attention. "I can try to get them back, but I can't do it alone."

The villagers only stared at him, fear in their eyes. And as his eyes made contact with theirs, they quickly looked away.

"Your loved ones and my friends have been taken," Tom stressed. "We can do something . . . *please*."

But they still ignored him, many going back to their homes and closing the doors firmly behind them. An overwhelming feeling of helplessness slowly came over Tom.

"I'm sorry, Tom."

He looked down to the ground to see Lorimar standing near his foot, her head bowed. "I'll go with you, but I'm not sure how much help I'll be in this state."

"The Chief." Tom turned toward the meeting house. "He has to do something. His daughter was taken."

The boy ran to the large double doors, flung them

open, and strode inside. "Chief Gnod," he said, about to tell the leader of his daughter's fate, but he could clearly see that the man and his wife already knew.

The Chief stood beside his chair, holding his crying wife in his arms. "Leave us be, boy," he ordered. "Leave us alone with our grief."

Tom stepped closer. "We have to do something, sir. Those things took my friend, too. If we put some men together we could go into the mountains and —"

"Those things have been coming to our village, picking away at us since we attempted to conquer Atheia." The Chief's face was flushed with emotion. "This is our fate," he said sadly.

"What are you saying?" Tom asked incredulously. "That you're supposed to just let this happen? That those bats taking away your daughter and other members of your village is your punishment?" Tom was getting madder by the second. He'd never heard such an excuse to sit and do nothing.

"Go away, boy," the Chief said with a wave of his hand. "You're free to go, for it appears with the taking of your small friend that you are as cursed as we are."

Tom actually started to leave the hall, but then his anger got the better of him. "I always heard that the men of Pawa were fearsome, hardy people who could survive the harshest of conditions . . . or at least *try* to." Tom made eye contact with the other warriors present. "Isn't there anyone here who will come with me?"

A few of them looked as though they were about to move forward, but they quickly lowered their gazes, stepping back into the crowd as Gnod glared at them.

"No one will be going with you," the Chief said. "We've already lost too much."

Tom couldn't believe his ears. "Look at you," he said, his voice filled with disgust. The Chief's men avoided his glance. "I'd trade a hundred of you for one Barclay Bone."

He waited for a response — something, anything — but they all remained silent, ashamed.

"Just so you know," Tom said, heading for the door. "I'm going to get my friend back, and your daughter, and anyone else I can save." He passed a large bearded man dressed in leather and heavy furs, a sheathed sword hanging from his side. He had been one of the few who had started to come forward. "Can I borrow that?" Tom asked him, pointing at the weapon.

The warrior hesitated, looking in the direction of his Chief.

"Wait," the Chief said. "You shame us, boy," he said sadly, suddenly looking older.

"Then you'll come with me?" Tom asked, looking

around the room, but still no one stepped forward.

"We were once brave warriors," the Chief began, "but now we are just shadows, bearing the burden of our guilt."

"I feel very sorry for you," Tom said, "but I need to do something." He put his hand out for the bearded warrior's sword.

"The least I can do is provide you with the means to protect yourself," Chief Gnod said, motioning for Tom to follow him.

Tom walked behind the Pawa leader to the back of the great hall, stopping before a large door.

"In here," Chief Gnod said, taking a metal key from his robes and unlocking the heavy wooden door.

The door opened with a whining creak, and he took a burning torch from the wall for light and led Tom inside. The room behind the door was an armory, filled to the brim with all manner of weaponry. There were swords — both long and short — battle-axes, spears, and armor.

"The Chieftain's arsenal," Gnod said, walking among the weapons. "Take whatever you think you might need."

Not being a warrior, Tom could only guess at what might be useful. In a large wooden chest, he found a vest of chain mail and removed it. "This might come in handy," he said, remembering the bat creatures' razor-sharp teeth and claws.

"An excellent choice," Gnod said, watching as Tom slipped the armor over his head. "That was made by our oldest blacksmith before his death, for the son that I never had."

"You could have given it to your daughter," Tom said, picking through a pile of very sharp-looking knives.

"A girl cannot be a warrior," the Chief said, but Tom recalled the fierceness of the brown-haired girl as she came to his aid against the flying beasts and knew that the Chief was wrong.

"If you say so," Tom said.

Chief Gnod held the burning torch higher so that the cache of weaponry was better illuminated.

"A sword," the older man said. "A true warrior needs a sword." He moved to a far wall where multiple swords hung from a rack bolted to the chamber's wooden wall. "Perhaps one of these," he said, reaching for a weapon.

Tom was about to move closer for a look when, from the corner of his eye, he saw a glow. A soft, warm light was emanating from behind another large wooden chest, and he found himself moving toward it.

He bent over the chest, craning his neck to see the source of the eerie light, and then noticed the muted glow coming from the Spark around his neck. It was still covered in the drying black spit of the bat monster, and he rubbed the filth away to allow the Spark to glow.

"What is it?" Chief Gnod asked, coming to stand beside him.

"I don't know," Tom said. "Something is glowing behind there."

The Chief grabbed the chest and slid it over to reveal a stack of old weaponry covered in layers of dust and thick cobwebs. The light was coming from somewhere among them. Tom reached down, the Spark around his neck dangling close to the other source of light, igniting them both in a brilliant flash.

The Chief gasped, jumping back.

But Tom was drawn to it, reaching into the stack of weaponry, his hand searching for something in particular. He knew he had found what he was searching for as soon as his fingers touched it.

The metal was warm and comforting to his touch.

Tom stood, bringing the weapon out from its hiding place. It was a short sword, and the way it felt in his hand, it was almost as if it had been made especially for him.

"I've never seen that sword before," Chief Gnod said.

Tom held the weapon before him, his face bathed in the light exuding from a polished stone placed in the hilt of the sword.

A stone that was actually a piece of the Spark.

"I think I was supposed to find this," Tom said, the

larger piece of the Spark around his neck glowing in unison with that of the sword's.

"I believe you were," Chief Gnod said, a touch of awe in his voice.

The Chief's daughter had no idea what her fate would be. All she knew was that two bat creatures, their leathery wings pounding the cold mountain air, were taking her and the little Bone that clung desperately to her foot to someplace unknown.

She had often wondered what happened to the poor souls that had been snatched from her village, and she guessed that she was soon going to find out.

Feeling Barclay's grip on her ankle begin to slip, Gerta craned her neck for a look down at the Bone that hung on for dear life. "Hold on!" she screamed over the wailing winds and flapping bat wings.

"I don't know if I can!" Barclay cried.

"Of course you can," she told him. She could feel his tiny hands fumbling around her ankles. "That's it," she said. "Get a good grip and hold on tight."

"What if they drop us?" Barclay cried.

"I don't think that's their plan," she replied. "If they were going to do that, I imagine they would have done it by now. They're taking us someplace, and you just need to hold on until we get there."

"I'll try," Barclay yelled. "But I don't know how long I can —"

"You can do it, Barclay," Gerta encouraged him. "Just listen to my voice."

"I'm listening, but I still don't know if —"

A powerful gust of freezing wind suddenly pummeled them, and she found herself flapping in the air like a sheet hung out to dry. Gerta could see the little Bone twisting below her, could feel his hold on her beginning to weaken.

"Barclay!" she cried out.

The little boy did not answer this time.

"Hang on, please," she begged. "I know it's hard, but I don't want to be alone. Don't make me be alone, Barclay."

Gerta wasn't quite sure, but she could have sworn that the little Bone's hold became that much tighter, and she hoped it would be enough until they reached their unknown destination.

Barclay's fingers were completely numb, and if somebody had told him that they'd broken off and blown away, he might have believed them, but he could still see them wrapped around the girl's ankle.

He didn't know for how much longer, though. The numbness was spreading. He could feel it moving through his hands, into his wrists, and up his arms. The wind wasn't helping matters either. At times it hit him so hard that it felt like he was being punched over and over by his sister.

Barclay didn't think it was possible, but at that moment, he actually missed Abbey and her punches, and wished that he could have been with her right then so she could hit him.

His stomach suddenly did a backflip, and he realized that they were descending — very quickly.

Barclay wasn't really sure if he wanted to see where they were, but he couldn't help himself and looked down to see a wall of mountain coming up on them fast. The little Bone squeezed his eyes tight, preparing for impact . . . but it didn't come.

Instead, he opened his eyes to pitch darkness, and the sensation of falling until his butt landed on the rocky ground with a jarring thud. Momentarily stunned, Barclay lay there, his tingling fingers gripping the ground beneath them. He wanted to be sure that it was actually there and not some kind of hallucination.

"We've landed," he said happily, temporarily forgetting their situation.

"We have," he heard Gerta say from somewhere nearby. "But where, exactly, I haven't any idea."

"I think we're in a cave."

Barclay's eyes started to adjust to the gloom, what little light there was barely making it down from the entrance they had flown through. He could just about see the girl's shape in front of him and made his way toward her.

"Are you all right?" he asked.

"I'm fine," she said. "And you?"

Barclay flexed his fingers. "Still a little prickly, but the feeling's coming back."

There was a fluttering sound that quickly grew louder and more frenzied, and Barclay realized that they were no longer alone. The bats seemed to be made out of something even blacker than the darkness of the cave, multiple sets of glistening red eyes appearing on all sides as the creatures landed around them.

"What do you think they want?" Barclay asked fearfully.

"I think we're about to find out," Gerta answered.

The bats surged forward with a hiss, flapping their large wings and driving the children farther into the darkness of the cave. They were forced down a sloping path that was illuminated by patches of glowing green moss. The passage eventually opened up into a much larger chamber, its ceiling high and hanging with what appeared to be long, dripping icicles.

"Wow, look at those," the little Bone said to Gerta as he pointed at the ceiling. "My uncle Percy says those are called stalactites."

But the Chief's daughter didn't hear him. She was staring far ahead into the gloom, at the multiple shapes that moved along what appeared to be a great wall of stacked stones of every conceivable size and shape.

"Hey, who are they?" Barclay asked.

"I believe those are the people taken from my village," Gerta said.

He was about to ask what they were doing when they were savagely struck from behind and knocked to the rocky ground.

"What'd you do that for?" Barclay yelled.

A chilling sound like laughter filled the chamber, and Barclay slowly rose to his feet, helping Gerta to stand as well.

The source of the disturbing noise was there before them, draped across what first appeared to be a tall pile of rocks, but on closer inspection turned out to be bones.

Hundreds and hundreds of bones.

It was another one of the bat creatures, only this one was at least twice the size of the others. And the way it looked at them, grinning horribly on its throne of bones, Barclay thought it appeared much smarter than the others.

And he was correct in this assumption, for the monster began to speak.

"Take them to the others," the leader of the evil bats commanded. "Put them to work!"

His bat minions swarmed about them, snapping their jaws and flapping their wings to drive them across the chamber toward Gerta's people.

And the enormous wall of rock that loomed before them.

Maybe being a turnip farmer isn't so bad, Tom thought as he carefully climbed up the mountain. *Maybe being a turnip farmer is the best job in the whole Valley.*

His foot slipped on a loose rock, and he slid roughly down the few feet that he'd just climbed, skinning his knee and causing a mini avalanche.

"Careful, Tom," Lorimar cautioned.

The weakened plant woman sat on his shoulder, her rootlike fingers wrapped through the links of the chain-mail vest he wore.

He'd been climbing for a few hours, and the sky was filled with gray undulating clouds that blotted out the position of the sun, and he couldn't tell the time of day.

Tom rested for a moment, remembering the sad faces of the Chief and his people as he had prepared to leave the village. It was as if the Nacht had somehow found his way into them, burrowing into their souls and filling them with darkness and taking away their hope.

He could feel it in the village — like a bad smell hanging in the air — and knew that if he'd hesitated much longer, that hopelessness would begin to affect him, too, and the quest would be over.

The Nacht would have won.

But the sword, with the polished fragment of the Spark glowing in its hilt, and the larger piece around his neck, would not let him succumb.

Maybe that's what the Spark is, he thought. *The Spark is the first ray of light that fought back the darkness of nothing, but maybe it's also hope.*

"We should continue on," Lorimar suggested, turning her gaze up into the thick clouds that swirled around the mountains above them.

Tom was thinking about staying put for a little bit longer, but felt the warmth of the stones. They had started to glow as if urging him on. Filling him with hope.

"Yeah," Tom said, turning to face the mountain once more. "The Chief said that the caves are at least a good day's climb away."

Chief Gnod had called out to him just as he had begun his journey, directing Tom to the mountain paths that were worn into the rock by the yearly migrations of mountain goats. The Chief had then shared the knowledge of the caves that honeycombed the mountain, and how perhaps this was where the monsters had taken his daughter, Tom's friend, and the other villagers.

Tom thought that he'd seen a little bit of something in the old Chieftain's eyes that hadn't been there before, that maybe the Spark had started a fire in the man — weak and barely there, but still burning nonetheless.

Tom had used this idea as inspiration to kindle his own fire, climbing steadily up into the cold, foreboding mountains. He'd reached a small plateau and was waiting for the wind to blow away some of the thick cloud cover so that he could get a better look at his surroundings, when he heard the ominous sounds of flapping wings.

"We must be getting close," Tom said, squinting into the clouds. At times he thought he saw movement within them and clutched the hilt of his sword.

"The Nacht is stronger here," Lorimar said cautiously. The plant woman climbed down from his shoulder, dropping to the ground. She knelt there as Tom crouched, waiting, and stuck her fingers into tiny cracks in the rock and what little dirt there was. "He poisons the air and even permeates the rock itself."

The sounds of multiple creatures in flight increased, growing closer by the second, but Tom was ready.

"Our time grows short, Tom," Lorimar warned.

He wanted to tell the plant woman that he knew how dire their situation was and he didn't really need to be reminded of it.

Especially now.

The first of the evil bats emerged from the shifting mist with a hiss and a flash of razor-sharp teeth.

Tom let out a scream, terrified by what was coming at him, but that didn't stop him from swinging his sword at the thing. He felt the sensation of the blade slicing through hairy flesh and leathery wing as the bat screeched in pain and surprise.

Its cry of agony drew other bat monsters, and they swarmed all around Tom as he pressed his back against the mountain so that they couldn't get at him from behind. Tom continued to swing his sword, driving his attackers away, taking strength from the Spark fragment that warmed his hand through the short sword's hilt.

"We can't stay here," Lorimar announced.

"What do you suggest?" Tom asked with a grunt, cutting through the face of a bat, its body dropping lifelessly to the ground before rolling over and down the mountainside.

"When I connected to the mountain I saw the caves," the plant woman said. "They're not too far above us."

The screeching bats were increasing, more and more of them being drawn to his efforts to fight them.

"So I'm guessing you think we should climb," Tom asked, swinging his sword through the thick mist to keep the monsters at bay.

"I think that would be best," she answered. "It won't be long until they completely swarm this location, and there will be too many for you to fight."

"Let's go," he said, quickly reaching down to pick up Lorimar and place her on his shoulder before beginning to scale the mountain once more.

He could hear the bat monsters screeching below them, communicating with one another as they looked for him. Tom tried to find a more solid grip, his foot loosening some pieces of rock that rolled down the mountain. Glancing over his shoulder, he was terrified to see that at least three of the evil bats had perched on rocks a couple yards away and were looking up at him with beady eyes.

Tom had no choice but to climb faster. The screeching and wailing from below had intensified, and he knew that they would be coming for him soon. He needed to find a place to make his stand, and find it quickly.

"Where were those caves again?" Tom asked, grabbing hold of a jutting piece of rock and hauling himself up.

"Close," Lorimar said. "But I'm not exactly sure how close."

Tom climbed up onto a flat section of mountain rock. There were bats in the air around him, swooping out of the mist, and there were bats below, dragging their misshapen bodies up the mountain in pursuit.

Things were not looking very good at that moment.

Tom felt panic creeping up inside him but tried to keep it at bay. If there was one thing that he had learned while on this quest, it was not to panic. He remembered Randolf's calmness during the most frightening aspects of their journey, how the Veni Yan had shown him that

part of survival was carefully thinking through dangerous situations with a level head.

One of the beasts came up over the slight edge, its clawed talons digging into the rock as it tried to drag itself up, and another three flew at him from the air.

Tom took a deep breath and slashed the short sword through the air, temporarily driving his air attackers back, and then brought the blade down on the crawling bat's clawed appendage. It lost its grip and fell backward onto the other climbing bats.

"I'm going higher," Tom announced, spinning around and clambering up the slight incline.

The fog was thicker there, and another bat flew at him, swooping out of the swirling gray, but Tom was ready. He cut through the air with his weapon and brought it down.

But that twisted creature seemed to have just been a distraction, as three more exploded at him from the opposite side. Tom turned to address the sudden attack, but he was too slow. The three bats knocked him to the ground and he rolled dangerously close to the edge.

Panic was back, loud and pounding in his brain and chest, but he would not let it take hold. *What would Randolf do?* he asked himself as he struggled to his feet.

At that moment, a bat leaped up from below and grabbed at him with horribly hooked claws. Tom struggled in its foul grasp, trying to drive it from his body, but the thing held on. The monster was too close, preventing him from using his sword. Tom stumbled back against a section of the rock wall to avoid an attack from behind, and the bat momentarily lost its grip. The bat tried to slash at him again, but its claws were ineffective against the vest of chain mail that he wore.

Lorimar left her perch on his shoulder. "I may be small and nearly powerless in this environment, but that does not mean I am useless," she said, landing on one of the bat's hairy limbs. Tom watched as the plant woman reached over and snapped off her right hand at the wrist.

"Lorimar, what are you . . . ?" Tom cried, but she didn't answer as she shimmied up the bat's body and, using the jagged end of her arm like a spear, drove it into the monster's face. It screamed in surprise and agony, flinging itself backward and away, tossing Lorimar to the ground.

But that did not end the escalating threat. The sky had become filled with bats, all of them searching for him.

"C'mon, Lorimar," Tom said as he reached down to scoop her from the ground, shoving her into the pocket of his tunic beneath the chain mail. "There are so many of those things right now, I can't imagine that the cave entrances are that much farther."

With a burst of reserved strength, Tom darted up a rocky path, moving higher still — a move that proved to be not the smartest.

Tom was suddenly out in the open, the shifting clouds moving in such a way to leave him totally exposed to his attackers. The bats moved en masse, like a giant cloud of blackness dotted with glimpses of red eyes and razor-sharp teeth. They were descending on him, and he stood ready, sword in hand.

"I need you to leave me if it looks like I'm not going to make it," Tom said.

"What do you mean?" Lorimar asked, pushing the chain mail aside to peek her head out.

"I need you to promise me that you'll try and help save Barclay and the Chief's daughter, and that you'll all try to find the others and finish the quest."

The cloud of bats swirled above his head like some chattering, screeching tornado of evil.

"Maybe if we climb a little more we could —"

"No more climbing," Tom said. "This is it. . . . Promise me."

The plant woman hesitated.

"Promise me," Tom demanded.

"I . . . I promise," Lorimar said.

With his free hand, Tom reached underneath the armored vest, took her from his pocket, and dropped her to the ground.

"Go," Tom told her, his eyes still on the growing number of bats. "Find the caves. Find Barclay and Gerta."

And then it happened: One long and terrifying cry escaped the cloud of bat monsters as one of them sharply changed its course. This was it.

And Tom was ready.

He raised his weapon, and the sun inexplicably came out — or at least he thought it was the sun.

A blinding light cut through the gloom, bathing the mass of flapping monstrosities in its brightness. The creatures cried out in torment, dispersing, their colony broken into individual beasts flying this way and that to escape the burning rays of light.

Tom stared up in wonder as the light that cut through the thick clouds wrapped around the mountains and chased away the flying vermin that would have surely ended his life.

"What is it?" Lorimar asked him.

He was about to tell her that he didn't know when he heard the familiar sound. An enormous smile filled his face as he watched the awesome sight of the *Queen of the Sky* slowly emerge from the churning clouds. Tom let out a cheer, raising his sword to the approaching craft.

Percival waved wildly from the deck of the craft, his potato-powered spotlight shining down on Tom. The Rats were there as well, Stinky waving excitedly with what remained of his dead squirrel.

"Hey ya, Tom," Percival called out. "Nice to see ya!"

Tom moved closer to the edge. "Are Randolf and Abbey with you?" he yelled.

The Bone explorer shook his head. "No, haven't found them yet."

Tom was excited to be reunited with Percival and the *Queen*, but he knew what needed to be done right then.

"Keep searching the mountains," he called up to the sky ship. "I need to go into the caves and find Barclay and a girl named Gerta." He could see the confusion on the Bone's face. "I'll explain it all when I get back. Just find the others!" he told Percival, already preparing to resume his climb for the caves.

"I'm going with you," Lorimar announced.

"Are you sure? You could grow yourself a new body up on the *Queen* and help Percival search for . . ."

"I'm going with you," the plant woman repeated. "I *need* to go with you."

"All right, then," Tom said, reaching his arm down to allow her to scramble up onto his shoulder again. "Let's get going."

With a final wave to the *Queen of the Sky*, he climbed up and up and up — which was easier to do now that the bats were gone — until he found an opening and went inside, swallowed up by the darkness.

CHAPTER 12

The Rats had found a scent.

The Constable watched as the filthy beasts followed the invisible trail with their faces pressed to the rocky ground.

"What is it?" he asked. "What have they found?"

King Agak joined his soldiers and sniffed. "They walked here not long ago," the Rat leader announced.

A spark of excitement jolted through the evil spirit's borrowed body. *Is this it?* he wondered. *Are we finally going to be able to prove ourselves?*

"Is it the boy?" the Constable asked, trying to keep his eagerness at bay. "Is it Tom Elm and the others?"

"No," the Rat King growled. He lifted his shaggy head and sniffed again. "Something else."

The Constable noticed the other Rats had also lifted their hairy faces to the sky, and then, one by one, they bounded up the hill.

But if it wasn't the boy and the other questers, then who
— or what — had the monsters found? The Constable was
growing more and more annoyed with the Rats. He motioned for his deputies to follow, and they scrambled up the
mountainside after the hungry beasts.

They found the Rats at the edge of a cliff, their fur-
covered rumps raised as if preparing to pounce.

"Wait!" the Constable ordered. "What is it? What have
you found?"

King Agak and the others turned toward him with ferocious snarls, their faces wet with drool. "Prey that does
not concern you," Agak proclaimed, looking back over the
cliff's edge.

"I'll be the judge of that," the Constable said with authority, moving among the Rats so that he could see what
they had found.

At first he noticed nothing, but on closer examination,
he saw two very small figures walking side by side up a
stone-covered path. The Constable wasn't impressed in the
least, but then he noticed the flaming arrow that hovered
in the air above the strange pair and realized that these
two — whoever they were — might be of importance.

"After them," the Constable ordered. "But do not harm
them in any way . . ."

The Rat King glared angrily.

"Yet," the Constable finished, and the Rat Creatures bounded over the cliff.

"Do you want me to carry you again?" Stillman asked Porter.

"No, I'm all right," the turtle answered as he walked by the Dragon's side.

"We've certainly lived an interesting life, haven't we?" Stillman asked his friend.

The turtle thought for a moment before answering. "You're probably right. I always forget that not everybody has had the kind of life we've had."

"And it ain't over yet," Stillman said. He picked up a rock and threw it up ahead of them. "Who knows what could be next?"

"I think I'm done after this," Porter said. "I'm getting too old for all this adventuring stuff."

"Ah, you're still a baby," Stillman said.

"For a Dragon, maybe, but I'm pretty ancient for a turtle."

"I guess," Stillman agreed. "But I hope you change your mind because it wouldn't be the same without you."

"Let's just get through this one and —"

A shower of small rocks rained down on them and the pair came to a stop.

"I don't think we're alone anymore," the little turtle said fearfully, searching the shadows with widened eyes.

"You're probably right," Stillman said. "I *thought* this trip had been awfully easy."

The Rat Creatures slunk down from the hills with a menacing hiss and circled them.

"See, this is what I mean," Porter said. "My old heart just can't take this sort of thing anymore."

Stillman watched as the Rats stared at them hungrily, but none of them made a move to attack. *Strange*, the Dragon thought, just before four more figures emerged from the shadows. They seemed to be human, but as Stillman looked closer and gazed into their eyes, he realized they were not.

"Oh, I see," the young Dragon said as one of the men stepped forward with a strange grin on his face.

"What do you see, Dragon?" the man asked.

"I see you," Stillman said, pointing at the man. "Behind those eyes, I see you hiding in there."

"What do you see, Stillman?" Porter asked.

"Spirits," the Dragon answered. "The evil kind. They're inside the men, controlling them. Now it makes sense that they and the Rats are together."

Bad has a habit of joining with bad, the Dragon thought.

"Can we eat them now?" one of the Rats asked the spirit leader.

"Patience, King," the spirit possessing the man with the curled mustache answered. "I need to know what brings such a young Dragon into these cold, forsaken mountains."

"None of your business," Stillman said. He sensed the malice oozing from the possessed humans, as well as the Rat Creatures, but he tried not to show any fear. The Red Dragon had said the reasoning behind why the Dreaming had chosen him for such an important task would become obvious over time, and he wondered if this was one of those reasons.

"No need to be rude," the possessed leader stated. He shared a mocking laugh with the others. "We were just curious as to what two small, defenseless creatures were doing up here in such cold, inhospitable conditions."

"I was gonna say that it had nothing to do with the likes of you guys," Stillman said, eyeing them all. "But now I'm not so sure."

"Did the Red Dragon mention anything about Rat Creatures?" Porter asked.

At the mention of the great Red Dragon, the Rat Creatures all hissed and the possessed men took a step back.

Red had that kind of effect on folks.

"The Red Dragon?" the possessed leader asked with a snarl. "What could the likes of you two pathetic things have to do with him?"

"I think you guys might be part of a problem he told

me about," the Dragon said as calmly as he could. He was nervous, his stomach doing all sorts of flips.

"Oh, you do, do you?" the leader asked. "And I think you might be part of *our* mission," he added.

"You're on a mission, too?" Porter asked. Stillman felt Porter poking his leg. "They're on a mission, too," the little turtle said from the corner of his beak.

"And I think our mission is to let the Rats have you, but to leave enough pieces behind to show anyone who might think of challenging the Nacht that their efforts would be fruitless."

The Nacht, Stillman thought. It was the first time that the evil they were facing was given a name. Helping to stop the Nacht — that was his mission. Things were becoming clearer now. Just like the Red Dragon had said.

The leader of the foul spirits gave a signal to the Rats, and they began to stalk toward Stillman and Porter. Stillman waited . . . waited for a sign.

A sign that would tell him what he should do.

The Rats were almost upon them, and Porter was screaming when it happened.

Something in Stillman's chest rumbled, and he could feel the fire inside him start to grow. At first he thought he might be sick, but then realized that it was something much more than that.

Was this what he had been waiting for?

The fire was churning in his belly like crazy, almost as if it knew something that he didn't.

Well, it is *special fire*, he thought, trying to relax in preparation for whatever was about to happen.

"Stand back, Porter," he warned his friend, gently pushing the turtle away.

The fire was building. It rose up in his throat, feeling so powerful that he thought he might explode if he didn't let it out.

So he did.

The flame rushed from his open mouth in an expanding plume of bright oranges and reds. The fire singed the Rats' fur, and they screamed, the air filling with an awful stink.

The Dragon momentarily pulled back on the fire as the Rats fled up into the mountains, leaving the possessed humans standing there in surprise.

Stillman could tell that this fire was even more different from usual, that it came from a different place inside him. Almost as if it had been stored away, saved for a special purpose.

Awakened by the strange stone that the Red Dragon had given him to swallow.

"Let's not be hasty," the possessed leader said, as he and the others carefully backed up. "We'll go our way, and you and your little turtle friend can go yours."

"I don't think so," Stillman said, feeling the special fire

beginning to rise again in his throat. "I don't think I'm supposed to let you go anywhere."

He tried to hold the fire back, but the flames leaped from his open mouth, engulfing the four men with the evil spirits inside them. Their cries were awful.

"Stillman, no!" he heard Porter yell, and the Dragon finally got control of his fire and pulled it back.

"You can't do that," the turtle said. "You can't just burn them."

"I know. I tried to keep it under control, but . . ."

Stillman chanced a look in the direction of the inhuman humans, to see what damage there might be. What he saw was completely unexpected.

"I didn't burn them," Stillman said in wonder, pointing.

The four men appeared fine. Their bodies were smoldering, but they weren't actually burning. They looked around, their eyes wide with surprise, almost as if they didn't know where they were.

"But I saw you breathe fire on them!" Porter said.

"I know," Stillman said, walking over to where the men were standing. Standing on the tips of his clawed toes, he looked into their faces and saw — or, more accurately, *didn't see* — something that amazed him.

"I didn't burn the men," Stillman said. "Just the evil that was inside them. My special fire burned away the evil!"

"So the evil is gone?" Porter asked, cautiously watching the men.

"*That* evil is," the Dragon said. "But there's still more where that came from."

The turtle looked around. "Like the Rat Creatures?"

"Nah, they're probably gone," the Dragon said. "We're not such an easy meal to them anymore."

The men were huddled together, fearfully looking around. Stillman was about to try and explain that they were all right, when their eyes grew wide and one of them pointed up into the sky.

The Dragon and the turtle turned to see the fantastic sight of a large wooden craft sailing out of the blowing mist.

"What is that?" Porter asked in awe.

The Dragon did not answer as it gradually drifted closer to them, a beam of light from aboard the ship illuminating them where they stood.

"Ahoy there!" said someone from the deck of the vessel.

Stillman started to smile as he got a better look at who was addressing them.

"Is . . . is that a Bone?" Porter asked.

"It certainly is," Stillman answered, feeling happy that he and Porter were no longer alone on their mission.

Help had arrived.

· · ·

In the land of the Dreaming, now totally besieged by darkness, the Nacht cried out in pain. He felt his connection with the evil spirits that served him in the Waking World sever. It was gone.

Burned away.

But how? the Dragon of shadow wondered, still reeling from the pain. *What could have done this?*

The Nacht rose to his feet before the wall of black that separated the Dreaming from the Waking World. He studied the wall, reaching out with his mind.

As far as he knew, the agents of the Dreaming were preoccupied with other tasks, distracted from their quest. Then who or what could have struck down his faithful servants?

As the Nacht's mind entered the roiling black clouds that blotted out the sun, he saw what shouldn't have been.

A Dragon.

A Dragon other than him was awake.

CHAPTER 13

The passage into the mountain cave was becoming more and more cramped. Tom lay on his belly in the pitch dark, squirming across the ground's rough surface, moving deeper into the narrow space.

"I'm not sure if this was such a good idea," he said to Lorimar as he squinted into the darkness, trying to see what lay ahead of him. There was nothing but black, and he began to worry that if the space got any tighter, he'd get stuck.

"Stay here," Lorimar said. "I'll see what's up ahead."

Tom could hear the sound of her spindly sticklike limbs as she scurried farther down the passage. He waited a moment, but his impatience got the better of him.

"Well?" he called out, wriggling a little farther down. He didn't think it was possible, but it seemed even darker now, and his anxiety began to rise. There was so much at stake, and somehow being in this tiny space made him acutely aware of that.

"Lorimar?" he called out again. Ahead of him an eerie glow began to manifest. It had a strange greenish coloring to it — not nearly as powerful as the brilliance thrown from the fragment of Spark, but it was enough to light his way. "Lorimar, is that you?" he asked.

He could see that the passage ahead of him opened up into a much larger chamber. He crawled forward, still clutching his sword, until the ceiling started to open up and he could rise to his knees. He ducked his head as he passed beneath a low-hanging section of rock and gasped at what he saw on the other side of it.

At first he thought it was some sort of ghost. He raised his sword, but then he realized that it was his friend.

"Is . . . is that you?" Tom asked.

"It is," Lorimar answered. She was full-sized again, and her body was made from a strange fuzzy plant, like mold on the trunks of old trees . . . only this mold glowed.

"This luminescent moss makes for an interesting form," she said, staring at her fuzzy, glowing hands.

"Now that you're full-sized again, let's see what we can do about finding Barclay and Gerta, and anybody else those bat things might've captured," Tom said as he strode toward the back of the chamber that he hoped would take them deeper into the mountains.

Lorimar's hand reached out, grabbing his arm as he passed.

"Wait," she whispered. She looked around as if sensing something near her.

"What is it?" Tom asked, raising his sword. "Is it the bats?"

He followed her gaze. It seemed to be growing darker in the cave, the shadows more solid and starting to converge upon them.

"Run, Tom," Lorimar said, standing perfectly still.

"I'm not going to run. What is it?" he asked, eyes darting from side to side. "We'll fight it together."

"No," she said firmly. "This I must face alone."

He was about to keep arguing when the plant woman suddenly turned and grabbed him by the arms. With a show of superhuman strength, she tossed him from the ever-darkening chamber.

Tom flew backward through the air, waiting for impact, but it did not come. He just continued to fall.

And fall, and fall.

"Do you think they're all right?" Abbey whispered to Roderick as they walked behind Randolf through the cave, their way illuminated only by patches of glowing moss. They were all following Roque Ja, traveling a winding path that sometimes climbed steeply and other times sloped deep down into the belly of the underground mountain range.

"I sure hope so," Roderick answered, knowing exactly who Abbey was asking about.

"Well, I think they're fine," the little Bone said confidently. "They're probably all together on board the *Queen* flying over the mountains looking for us."

"How will they find us down here?" Roderick asked.

"Don't worry," Abbey reassured him. "They'll keep looking until we come above, or maybe Uncle Percy will launch an expedition and they'll come down here to find us."

"That would be amazing," Roderick said.

"Yeah," she agreed.

The two fell silent as they continued to follow Randolf and the giant cat.

"I miss my brother," Abbey finally said.

"Yeah, and I miss Tom," Roderick responded.

"I miss my uncle, too," Abbey added. "Do you miss Lorimar?"

"I guess," the raccoon answered. "Even though she is sorta creepy."

"Yeah, but what would you expect from a plant lady? How about Stinky and Smelly?" She stifled a laugh.

"Don't even get me started on those two," Roderick said.

"Shhhhhhhhh!" Randolf shushed, turning around to glare at them. "We must be quiet in case more of those bat creatures are lurking about."

"Sorry," Abbey whispered as Roderick placed a paw over his mouth.

The mountain cat came to a stop up ahead, and Randolf, Abbey, and Roderick carefully approached him. Roque Ja had lowered his great bulk to the ground and was peering over the side of a cliff, his thick tail swishing agitatedly from side to side.

"Do you see something, Roque Ja?" Abbey asked cautiously. She squatted beside the cat and looked out at the vast, open chamber below.

"Yes, I see something," Roque Ja answered. "But I'm not sure what."

Randolf and Roderick joined them, and they all stared at the activity below. There were people there, all lined up along a section of the rock wall, hauling stones of all sizes and shapes under the watchful eyes of many bat creatures.

"What are they doing down there?" Roderick asked.

"It appears that the bats have them working," Randolf observed.

"Yeah," Abbey agreed, watching as the folks below carried the rocks to the center of the chamber and discarded them. "It looks like they're trying to take down that wall."

"But why?" Roque Ja asked.

And then Abbey's eye caught a flash of skin in the murky darkness below, skin far whiter than that of the people who worked there. "Hey, wait a minute," she said, excitement in her voice, as she leaned farther over the edge.

Roderick grabbed the back of her dress to keep her from falling. "What are you doing?" he asked.

Randolf reached down and pulled her back. "Abbey, you must be careful," he admonished.

But the little Bone wasn't listening, for she had caught sight of the most amazing thing, and she knew then that everything would be all right.

She had seen her brother.

"Hey, Barclay!" she suddenly cried out, her enthusiasm bubbling out of her. "We're up here!"

As one, the workers and bats below turned their eyes to the shadows above the chamber.

"Whoops," Abbey said as the shrieks of the bat monsters filled the air. "I probably shouldn't have done that."

"You two, over there," Percival ordered, pointing Susie the Blunderbuss at the turtle and, if he remembered correctly from the descriptions the Bone cousins — Fone Bone, Smiley Bone, and Phoney Bone — gave in their stories about the Valley, what looked to be a Dragon.

"What's he pointing at us?" the turtle asked his companion.

"Don't know," said the Dragon. "Could be some kind of weapon."

"It's a weapon, all right," Percival said with as much

conviction as he could muster. Even though the blunderbuss wasn't loaded, he had to make it look as though it was, and that it — and he — could do some serious damage if they wanted to. "And if you know what's good for you, you won't make me use it."

The Constable was next to come up the ladder and over the side. The man didn't look half as threatening as he had before. His three deputies followed. They all looked very lost . . . and very afraid.

"You four get over there with your buddies until I figure out what's going on around here."

Stinky and Smelly scrambled across the deck, peering over the side of the *Queen*.

"Was that the King I just saw?" Stinky asked, nervously petting what little remained of his squirrel.

"I think it was," Smelly answered. "First Rock Jaw, and now this!"

"Pipe down, you two!" Percival shouted, not wanting to take his eyes from his prisoners, even for a split second.

The turtle quickly ducked for cover, his head and limbs disappearing inside his shell as it clattered to the ship's deck. "Look out, Stillman!" the turtle shrieked from inside his shell. "Rats!"

"You don't need to worry about those two," Percival said, still looking down Susie's barrel at the four men and two little creatures.

"And you don't need to worry about us," the Dragon said, knocking on his friend's shell, urging him to come out.

"Yeah, well, I have my doubts about those four," Percival said, eyeing the Constable and his deputies.

The turtle had emerged, but was now peeking out from behind the Dragon.

"They won't give you any problems, Mr. Bone," the Dragon said. "I burned the bad right out of them."

Percival stared hard at the four men. "Is that true?" he asked.

"Please . . . we just want to go home," the Constable sniveled, and the others nodded in agreement.

"See, no more evil spirits," Stillman said proudly, crossing his little arms in front of his chest.

Percival slowly lowered the weapon. "How about that," the Bone adventurer said.

"What are you doing?" Smelly asked him in a panic. "Don't you know that's a Dragon?"

"I can see what he is," Percival said. "And I don't think he and his buddy mean us any harm."

"That's what they want you to think," Stinky said, leaning in close to whisper loudly in his ear. "And when your guard is down, they have you!"

Percival ignored the Rat, instead thinking of how odd it was that in the middle of nowhere, they had run into a

Dragon with the ability to burn away evil.

As if it was happening for a very specific reason.

"You fellas interested in being part of a quest?" Percival asked with a smile.

"Funny, I already thought we were on one. My name is Stillman," the Dragon said, turning his head and looking out over the side. "This is Porter," he continued, as the little turtle came out from behind his legs. "And I think we're supposed to go that way," he added.

Percival looked to where the Dragon was pointing, amazed to see an arrow of flame hanging in the sky.

"I think you're right," the Bone adventurer said, heading for the wheelhouse. "And the *Queen* is going to get us there."

CHAPTER 14

The darkness stole her away, ripping her from the body of glowing moss and dragging her spirit into the realm of the Nacht.

The first thing Lorimar heard was the screams of her people. Then the great Dragon of shadow was there before her, the sphere of the Dreaming that contained the survivors of the First Folk clutched in his taloned grip.

"Where is it?" the Nacht demanded, plumes of darkness trailing from its flaring nostrils.

"Patience, great Dragon," Lorimar tried to say in a soothing voice. "I have not yet had the opportunity to —"

"Make the opportunity," the Dragon bellowed. The sharp sound of something cracking, like winter ice during the time of thaw, echoed through the place. She saw jagged fractures appear on the sphere the Dragon held in his claws.

Her people wailed in fear, and the Dragon loomed menacingly closer.

"Bring it to me now," the Nacht demanded. "Before it is too late . . . for the ones you love."

Lorimar sensed something different then, saw it in the way the great beast of darkness carried himself. How agitated he seemed.

She was zapped back to the Waking World before she could give it more thought, only an instant having passed since she'd hurled Tom away. She reached out with her mind, touching the wild patches of glowing moss that grew throughout the cave system — and she found him, falling at a dangerous rate, deep down into a tunnel passage.

She sought out the closest patch of the thick, moist moss, and set to work growing a new form for herself, quickly spreading out over the ground where the boy would land. Just in time, Tom hit the mattress of moss with a grunt and the clatter of metal on rock as the short sword that he carried flew from his hand. The boy moaned as he rolled atop her.

Lorimar willed a new body to grow from the moss, then crossed the cavern floor to where the sword had fallen. The piece of the Spark from its hilt had broken free, and now lay glowing on the ground. Staring down at the stone, she heard the screams of her people. She bent down to retrieve the stone before returning to the boy.

"Lorimar?" Tom asked, dazed.

She knelt down beside him as he sat up. "Yes, Tom, it's me," she said, her eyes going to the nearly complete Spark that he wore around his neck.

She brought the newest piece of the solidified light toward the larger part that hung by the leather thong. It was pulled from her hand and then came a blinding flash as the lesser piece became part of the whole. Lorimar raised one of her mossy arms to protect her eyes from the explosion of light, and as she brought her arm down, she bore witness to another amazing sight.

Not only did the Spark around Tom's neck glow radiantly, but so did the boy himself.

"Wha . . . what's happening?" Tom asked, gazing at the pulsing light emanating from his body.

All Lorimar could do was stare, for she did not know the answer.

Stillman balanced on top of the *Queen of the Sky*'s steering wheel, staring intently through the cracked wheelhouse windows, searching for a sign. He could feel in his belly that they were getting close.

Either that or he shouldn't have eaten those old gooseberries that Porter found inside his shell.

Percival Bone jerked the wheel slightly in order to follow the flaming arrow through the shifting mists, and Stillman had to do a little dance to keep his place on the curve of the wheel.

"Sorry about that," Percival said. "How are we doin'?"

The Dragon felt his belly rumble and quickly placed his hand on it, feeling it bubble and churn. "Good, I think," he answered, watching the arrow as it temporarily disappeared into the wispy clouds before appearing again. The winds coming off the mountains were fierce, and it was taking all that the Bone navigator had to keep the sky ship on course.

"So what exactly are we looking for?" Percival asked, gripping the wheel tightly.

"I'm not sure, really, but I think I'll know it when I see it."

"I hope so," the Bone answered.

A few minutes of silence followed as both concentrated on the flaming arrow in front of them and Percival tried to keep the vessel flying straight.

"So you're really a Dragon, eh?" Percival said, breaking the silence.

"Yep, and you're a Bone."

"I certainly am."

"Have you ever met Big Johnson Bone?"

"He's a distant cousin, but nope, never had the pleasure," Percival answered. "He was a bit before my time, I'm afraid. But he's one of the reasons why I do what I do."

"Fly a sky ship?" Stillman asked.

"Exactly," Percival said. "Fly a sky ship and explore

the world . . . discovering things that nobody else has ever seen."

Stillman smiled. He believed that Big Johnson would have liked this Percival Bone.

Suddenly, through all the gloom there was a flash.

"Whoa!" the little Dragon cried.

The explosion of light was brief, but it left an impression as it temporarily dispersed the churning clouds to reveal the rocky mountains below and the source of the flash.

Porter appeared at the doorway of the wheelhouse. "Did you see it, Stillman?" he asked excitedly.

"I did," the Dragon replied, watching as the gray fog covered the mountains yet again. "Could you bring us to a stop right here, Percival?"

"Sure can." Percival pulled on some ropes connected to valves above his head and turned a few knobs on the panel before him, and Stillman felt the craft's forward momentum come to a gradual stop.

"So what now?" Percival asked.

"I'm not sure about you guys," Stillman answered, jumping to the floor. He walked outside onto the deck, where the Constable and his deputies sat huddled under the watchful eye of the two suspicious Rat Creatures. "But I think I'm supposed to go down there," the Dragon said, pointing down into the churning mist. The fire in his gut had started to bubble and churn like crazy.

"Give me a second and I'll join you," Percival said, letting go of the wheel. The *Queen of the Sky* began to rock as the winds tried to take hold.

"On second thought . . ." Percival said, grabbing the wheel and trying to keep the craft steady.

"No worries," the little Dragon said. "I think I'm supposed to do this part alone anyway."

Porter approached his friend. "You don't want me to come along?"

Stillman reached out to pat his friend's bald turtle head. "Sorry, but not this time, buddy," he told him.

Everyone on board the *Queen* was watching him, and he wished he could bring them — adventure was a lot more fun with friends. But in this case, it was most definitely a no-go.

"Be careful, then," Porter told him.

"I will."

"And if you see my niece and nephew, tell 'em that I'm looking for 'em!" Percival hollered.

"If you run into any other Rat Creatures, tell them that you've never seen us," Smelly said.

"Or Fredrick," Stinky added.

Rat Creatures are gross, Stillman thought.

"Wish me luck," the little Dragon said. He then spread the leathery wings beneath his arms and jumped from the deck, gliding down through the cool mist and toward the sign that had beckoned to him in the form of a beautiful burst of light.

The sound of Abbey's screechy voice was enough to bring all work on the wall to a complete stop.

But it couldn't possibly be her . . . could it? Barclay was still in a state of shock after what he and Gerta had been through. They'd been roughly tossed before the enormous wall of rocks, forced to work with the others under the watchful eyes of those nasty bat creatures.

Gerta had been so excited to see the people from her village that she'd called out to several by name, but they had simply stared at her with blank eyes, none of them slowing their work.

Barclay learned why the poor people hadn't stopped when a pair of bat creatures came rushing up behind them, lashing their leathery wings at their backs. It had hurt bad enough for Gerta and Barclay to quickly copy the other captives and pull large boulders from the wall, slowly taking it apart rock by rock.

But why? Barclay wanted to ask some of the others and gradually moved close enough to speak to one of the men, but when he saw the little Bone approaching, the man had shaken his head in warning and continued to work.

It was not until an old woman, who tirelessly used a jagged piece of rock as a tool, freed a large section of stone that Barclay got a clue that there might be something dangerous on the other side. The old lady let out a short squeak of a scream, and he and Gerta looked up from their work in time to see a wisp of smoke flow out of a crack in the wall and into the woman's face.

She fell heavily to the cave floor, fast asleep.

Just like the poor villagers we found on our quest to stop the Nacht, Barclay thought, an icy chill running down his spine as he watched the strand of darkness twist in the air, as if searching for someone else to put down, before it gradually dispersed. His eyes had been on that disintegrating tendril of darkness when Barclay heard that oh-so-distinctive voice.

"Hey, Barclay! We're up here!"

The little Bone turned and looked upward, his eyes searching the shadows of the vast chamber.

"Who is that?" Gerta asked.

"I think it's my sister!" he said, his gaze finally falling on the sight of his twin, who was high up on a ledge, jumping up and down and waving her arms.

"Yep, it's her."

Gerta was looking now, too, as were their bat guards.

"Is she alone?" Gerta asked as one of the bat monsters hissed at them threateningly.

Barclay could see the others up there with her, feeling a thrill as he recognized Randolf and Roderick. "Looks like

a couple of my friends from the quest are with her," he said proudly.

Then another shape peered out over the expanse of cave, and Gerta gasped. "Roque Ja."

But Barclay was distracted by the bats. They were furious that their chamber had been invaded, that the work had stopped, and more of the creepy things were flying in to help deal with the intruders.

"Think your friends might want to get out of here?" Barclay asked Gerta as he bent down to pick up one of the stones he'd dislodged from the wall. Gerta looked at him strangely.

The bats came at them, hissing and snapping their jaws, beating the air with their wings.

"What's that?" asked Barclay. "You say you need a rock? Well, here ya go!"

He threw the stone, hitting one of the evil bats square in the face. It squeaked pathetically, some of its teeth flying into the air before it collapsed to the ground in a twitching heap.

The other bats stopped for a moment, staring at their unconscious brethren, before turning back and advancing with even more anger.

But what Barclay had hoped for happened. The air was suddenly filled with flying stones of all sizes, pelting the bats and driving them back.

"This little boy shows us what true bravery is," said an old man with one jagged tooth in his mouth.

"Do as he does!" cried another, a heavyset man with a huge white beard that reminded Barclay of Santa Bone.

He reached down for another rock, as did Gerta and the people from her village, ready to fight back against their captors.

Inspired by the actions of a little Bone.

"Abbey, what were you thinking?" Randolf asked in a loud whisper, but it was already too late, the bat creatures were alerted to their presence.

"It's Barclay — he's down there!" the little Bone girl said, pointing to the cave floor below. She began to jump up and down and wave her arms. "Do you think he heard me?"

"I believe that everybody — and everything — in this cave heard you, which will be a problem," Randolf said, listening to the echoing, high-pitched shrieks of the monstrous bats.

The Veni Yan priest quickly peered at the ruckus below. He could see hundreds of the vile creatures taking to the air in a terrifying swarm of black.

"We're going to need to get off this ledge and find cover before —"

"But what about Barclay?" Abbey interrupted, panicked.

"We'll come up with a plan to reach him," Randolf said, pushing the little Bone and raccoon in front of him. "But right now, we must find a place to hide."

Roque Ja had already started to leave, and Randolf and the others ran to catch up.

"Where do you think you're going?" the great mountain cat asked with a ferocious snarl as he whipped around.

"We're leaving. . . . We're all leaving," Randolf said.

"I'm going this way," the great cat corrected. "You're going in some other direction. I had no interest in stirring up these . . . *things* . . . but now you've done just that."

"These *things*, as you call them, have everything to do with a great evil that will soon claim this Valley, and that includes your precious mountains," Randolf tried to explain as quickly as he could.

"I don't involve myself in matters such as this," the cat grumbled.

"Ignore them at your own risk," Randolf said, pulling Abbey and Roderick closer to him. "Or we can deal with them together."

Roque Ja considered his words, the shrill sounds of the bats nearly deafening as their cries reverberated through the cavern.

"I should have eaten you all when I had the chance," the mountain cat snarled. He turned away and padded quickly across the ledge toward another cave opening.

Randolf pushed the children and Roderick ahead of him, moving them along just as the first of the bats arrived, fluttering about and emitting the most earsplitting of cries. Roque Ja was just about to duck through the opening when Randolf saw the great cat suddenly recoil.

And then he saw it himself, far larger than any of the other loathsome bat creatures they had seen. The Veni Yan immediately knew that they had found the leader of these twisted beasts.

Or more correctly, it had found them.

"There you are," the leader said, surprising Randolf with its vocal capabilities. It crawled out from the confines of the tunnel, its beady red eyes fixed upon them.

Roque Ja backed away, and Randolf grabbed Abbey and Roderick, ready to take them back the way they had come, when he saw that more of the smaller bats were crawling toward them with murderous intent.

"We can't go back," Randolf announced, already drawing the sword at his side.

"Who said anything about going back?" Roque Ja asked, just before springing at the bat creature leader with a ferocious roar.

CHAPTER 15

Lorimar was compelled to touch it, to place her hand upon the Spark.

"What . . . what's happening to me?" Tom asked as she brought her mossy hand closer to the object around his neck.

She ignored his questions, hesitantly putting her green fingers on the smooth surface of the nearly complete Spark.

The connection was instantaneous. As soon as her fingertips touched the glowing surface, she was transported back. Back to that moment, when light declared its existence, and the darkness swore that it would never yield.

However, yield it did, for it could not contain the blessed life brought on by the explosion of light that birthed the Dreaming. But as the dark retreated farther and farther into the void of nothingness, it swore that there would come a time. A time when it would emerge to challenge the light once again.

And the powers that be accepted this and set a plan in motion.

Lorimar watched in awe as the fragments of Spark were sent out into the Waking World, secreted away, only to be found when the time was right.

Only to be found by one who was special enough to know.

One that would make the Spark whole.

And suddenly Lorimar understood it all.

She removed her hand from the Spark and returned to the Waking World. Even though the light from Tom's body had dwindled to a faint glow, she now saw better than if the sun was shining down upon them.

Tom was unconscious again, lying on the cold ground of the cave. She could hear the shrieks and cries of the bats and was considering moving the boy away from harm, when she caught the sound of something drawing closer in the darkness beyond them.

Lorimar turned toward the sound and saw a soft, orange glow illuminating a jagged opening in the wall of the chamber, glowing brighter as it approached.

"Hello?" called a voice, and Lorimar watched in wonder as a tiny Dragon crawled from the fissure into the cavern.

"Hi, I'm Stillman," the small Dragon said when he saw Lorimar standing in the center of the chamber. "And I'm here to do something very important."

. . .

Tom had returned to the darkness.

He floated there, in the warm, comforting embrace of shadow.

Waiting.

He felt no fear, instinctually knowing that this was part of a memory.

The memory of a past hidden from him.

He recognized a comforting, rhythmic sound and realized that he was back at the beginning.

His beginning.

Ba-Thump. Ba-Thump. Ba-Thump. Ba-Thump. The sound of his mother's heartbeat.

But then came a voice, and the darkness of the womb was filled with warm light and images of the most beautiful place, lush with the green of life.

"The darkness stirs," said the voice of the Dreaming. *"And a time may come when the Spark will be needed once more to drive back the hungry dark."*

Tom saw it all again, as if it was the first time, reveling in the Dreaming's attention.

"If needed, you will be my bearer of light," the Dreaming cooed. *"The final piece that makes the whole."*

The familiar darkness returned as the light receded.

"Go now into life."

• • •

Tom awakened with a cry. The Dreaming had chosen him, picked him as the one to fight for her. It was all making an odd kind of sense now: long before the frightening dreams of a place that seemed familiar but where he'd never been, before meeting Lorimar in the woods, and before finding what turned out to be that first fragment of Spark in the center of the largest turnip he'd ever seen.

He had been chosen.

"I understand," Tom said, getting to his feet. "Lorimar, I under . . ."

He stopped when he saw that something else was now in the chamber with them.

"That's good," said the strange, orange-skinned creature that could very well have been a . . . *Dragon*!

"Wouldn't want you to be scared of what I'm about to do," the Dragon said, crossing the cave to stand before Tom.

"What . . . what are you going to do?" Tom asked, taking a step backward.

"A big red friend told me a long time ago that I would know when I was supposed to do something special . . . something unusual," the little Dragon said. "And this is the time."

Before Tom could ask what he was going to do, the creature opened his mouth and took in a huge lungful of air.

And breathed fire on him.

Lorimar's eyes of mossy green bulged in terror.

The Dragon . . . this Stillman . . . had just belched fire upon the boy. Without thinking, she lunged across the rocky chamber.

"What have you done?" she wailed, roughly pushing the Dragon aside and throwing herself onto Tom's burning body.

"I ignited the Spark!" Stillman said excitedly. "So *that's* what the Red Dragon was talking about."

Lorimar heard the words but did not really listen to them, her concern being Tom Elm beneath her. She willed her body of moss to grow thicker and pulled as much moisture from the air as she could in hopes of suffocating the flames that burned his flailing body.

But the fire would not go out. In fact, it seemed to be growing brighter and stronger.

"It's all right!" the Dragon called out. "The boy will be fine."

Lorimar chanced a look at Tom and saw the most fantastic of things. Yes, the boy was covered in flames, but he did not burn, and she came to realize that neither did she. His skin, his hair, his clothes — they were all perfectly fine.

He wasn't on fire . . . he *was* the fire.

"Tom," she said, trying to avoid his thrashing fists. "You're unharmed!"

He continued to fight her, screaming out in fear, but his struggles lessened as he realized that she was right.

Lorimar removed herself from him, going to stand beside the little Dragon that watched from a safe distance.

"I told you he'd be fine," Stillman said, his yellow eyes reflecting the light thrown from the burning boy.

"Yes, you did," Lorimar said, not taking her eyes from the boy.

Tom looked at himself, studying the fire that emanated from his hands, licking hungrily at the darkness that was all around them. "Lorimar, I'm all right," he said, and he climbed to his feet. "Look at me, I'm all right."

And it all made a wonderful kind of sense as she watched him standing there before her. The Dreaming had explained it to her, but she hadn't been smart enough to understand. She'd been too wrapped up in her own misery to truly see what it had been trying to say, what it had been trying to show her.

Tom grasped the stone about his neck, and the light thrown from his body began to burn even brighter.

She hadn't understood what it all meant until now, until the Dragon's fire had awakened it.

Tom was the final piece of the Spark, and now it was truly complete.

. . .

The fear was burning away.

Just a moment ago, Tom had thought he was dead, that a Dragon had spit fire upon him and he would be burned away to nothing but ash and blackened bone.

But that wasn't what had happened at all.

The fire was hot at first, but as he became less afraid, the heat became less intense. These flames were different, special, and they not only touched the outside of his body but were on the inside as well.

It was then he realized that the Dragon's flames were part of the Spark, too, igniting the last piece that had lain dormant inside him since before he was born.

Taking hold of the Spark that hung around his neck, which was now connected to his inner light, he felt his body swell with the power of the primeval flash.

Totally aware of the magnitude of darkness rushing in to drown the world and how it was up to him to stop it.

The air was filled with monsters. They swarmed around Randolf and his charges as they struggled from the ledge to the floor of the cave.

"Stay close to me!" the Veni Yan ordered, slashing out with his sword when one of the furred nightmares got too close.

They were following Roque Ja. The great mountain cat had pounced on the largest of the bat creatures, both of them tumbling from the ledge and now battling on the cave floor below.

Randolf, Abbey, and Roderick carefully made their descent, pressing themselves close to the rock wall as the evil bats tried to pluck them away.

"Skreeeeeeeeeeeeeeeee!" one of the demon bats screamed. Flapping its thick, leathery wings to keep its misshapen body aloft, it took hold of Randolf's sword arm with one of its clawed feet, attempting to pull him from the wall.

"I've got you, Randolf!" Abbey Bone cried, grabbing hold of one of his legs, adding her weight to his.

Randolf could feel himself being pulled away from the wall, and just when he felt that the bat was going to have its prize . . . a rock struck the bat just above the eye, the force of the blow stunning the nightmare beast and causing its grip to falter. Roderick was readying his next throw as Randolf pulled his arm from the bat's clutches.

"Excellent throw," the Veni Yan praised the raccoon, just as the monster recovered and flew at them again. But this time, Randolf was prepared, burying his blade in its fur-covered belly.

The bat cried out, dropping from the air to land on a sharp outcropping of rocks below, but they were far from safe. Randolf slashed with his sword at the bats that continued to attack as Roderick and Abbey tossed rocks with uncanny precision.

Until the ledge they walked on suddenly came to an abrupt end, and there was nothing but a fifty-foot drop to the cave floor below them.

"Why are you stopping?" Abbey asked from behind Randolf.

Roderick continued with his barrage of rocks, stopping only when he ran into Abbey's back.

"What gives?" the raccoon asked.

"It appears we've run out of ledge," Randolf said.

"What are we gonna do?" Abbey asked as she picked up a rock and threw it at a bat that had gotten too close. "We can't just stay here waiting to get picked off."

An idea flickered in Randolf's brain. It was a crazy thought, but it was the only thing he could think of to get them to the ground in one piece.

"I want you both to climb onto my back," he said to Abbey and Roderick, already bending down.

"Why?" Abbey wanted to know.

"Do it!" he ordered, and the little Bone complied, hopping onto his back and wrapping her tiny arms around his neck. Roderick was right behind her.

Randolf stood with a grunt. "And before you say anything," he said. "I am well aware that this is completely insane."

Without another word, the warrior priest tensed the muscles in his legs as a particularly large bat flew past. He sprang from the ledge, sailing through the air to land atop the bat.

The bat's cries mingled with Abbey's and Roderick's terror-filled screams as it furiously pounded its wings, trying to stay aloft with the extra weight. But ever so slowly, it sank toward the ground, exactly as Randolf had anticipated.

Once they were close enough to the cave floor, the warrior priest let go of the monster, and it flew off in a complete panic.

"Remind me never to do that again," Abbey said, letting go of Randolf's back.

"That was just crazy," Roderick said with a shake of his head. "Kinda fun, but still crazy."

A roar followed by an ear-piercing cry of pain made them all turn in time to see Roque Ja, his fur matted with blood, ripping into the throat of the giant-sized bat he had pinned to the ground.

"That's gross," Abbey said.

"Yes," Randolf responded, his eyes at the far end of the darkened cave where the villagers were in the midst of battling the bat creatures. "I think they could use our help," he said to the great cat.

Roque Ja lifted his bloody face to look at the battle on the other end of the chamber and then went back to feeding on his fallen foe.

"They seem to be doing just fine," the cat grumbled.

There wasn't any time for arguments, so Randolf decided to just leave the mountain cat there for now.

"Well, if you care to join us, we'll be fighting the bats in an attempt to save the world from nightmares." The Veni Yan hurried across the cave with Abbey and Roderick.

"How thrilling for you," Roque Ja said, licking gore from his whiskers with a thick pink tongue as he watched them go.

"We need to stand together!" Gerta cried out, desperate to dispel the fear and panic that she saw in the eyes of her people.

"But there are so many of the monsters," a frightened old woman wailed, placing her hands on her head. Others protested as well. They were losing hope.

The bat creatures swooped down, picking up villagers who screamed and cried out in their grasp as they were carried up toward the ceiling.

"They're too scared," Barclay said, taking aim at one of the many bats that fluttered around in the air before them and letting a rock fly. "We've got to show them that working together will help us all." He gestured for the girl to pick up a rock as well.

Gerta snatched one up and threw it. Her rock hit a bat just under the wing and actually dropped it from the air.

The villagers looked at her then, and seeing that she

had their attention, she urged them to act.

"Fight them," she said, picking up another rock. "Show them that we are not going to do their bidding anymore."

She and Barclay threw their rocks together, and one by one she saw that her people were starting to motivate. The bats continued to swoop down upon the weakened villagers, but they were no longer easy targets. Gerta's people were starting to fight back, the rocks that they had worked so hard to remove from the great wall providing the ammunition they needed.

"That's it!" Gerta cheered as the rocks flew.

But the swarm was getting heavier, and the villagers began to falter as more of them were carried off by the bats.

"We need to get together," Barclay said. "We need to form a circle so they can't take any more of us."

"Together now!" Gerta cried, motioning for everyone to join her. In a matter of seconds, the villagers had formed a solid mass, each of them wielding rocks as weapons. As the bats dove down, they all lashed out at their attackers, savagely striking at the monsters' clawed feet and underbellies.

"That's it!" Gerta said. "Stay together!"

They thought that they might have had a chance until the bats started to use their own twisted brains, picking up rocks of their own and dropping them on their tight-knit numbers. Some were knocked unconscious, and the ones who fled were chased by the bats and carried off.

"We can't stay like this much longer," Barclay said, watching for swooping bats and falling rocks.

Gerta's eyes scanned the expanse of the cave, searching for someplace they might go for cover, but the distance was too great — they would be picked off with ease before they could reach their destination. And then she saw them: a man in the familiar robes of a Veni Yan priest, another little Bone, and a raccoon — all running toward them.

And behind them, moving at a more leisurely pace, the great mountain predator known as Roque Ja.

"Barclay, look," Gerta said, jabbing the Bone with her elbow.

He smiled as he watched the trio draw nearer. "I was wondering when they'd get here." He waved his arms above his head. "And it's about time, too. I thought we were just about done for."

Just then, there was a sound like the thunder of the worst spring storm, a vicious rumbling that caused their flesh to tingle and itch.

"What the . . . ?!" Barclay cried out, almost losing his balance.

The wall was shaking, loose rocks tumbling from weakened spaces, holes opening at random. The wall was coming down.

CHAPTER 16

Something wasn't right — the Nacht could feel it.

The shadow Dragon reared up from his bed made from those locked in nightmare and sniffed the inky blackness of the air.

"What is that?" he grumbled.

Evil spirits flew about his head.

"Can you feel it?" one asked.

"I can. . . . I can feel it," answered another.

The Nacht stood quickly, his awesome bulk moving toward the wall of shadow. It was there that he sensed it, there on the other side.

It was the power that he had been hunting for all this time. The power that, once in his possession, would allow nothing to stop him.

"Why aren't you here?" the Nacht growled, sensing the

Spark on the other side of the barrier that separated the world of shadow from the Waking World.

A wall of stone built to obstruct the Valley's largest Ghost Circle.

The Dragon pounded his fist on the wall. "Why aren't you here with me now?"

The power continued to thrive on the other side, and that just made the great Dragon all the angrier. After all that he had done, to have it be so close and still not be his.

It was maddening.

The Nacht reached beneath one of his wings and withdrew the special bubble he had tucked away there. The dirty and cracked sphere of Dreaming, the last First Folk still contained within.

"Why hasn't your savior brought it to me?" the Dragon asked the sphere. Those imprisoned inside cowered before his looming presence, as they should. Everyone should fear him, and they would, when the world was black and belonged entirely to him.

The Nacht spun in anger, slamming his muscular tail against the barrier. He could feel it give ever so slightly, but still not enough to tumble down, allowing his beautiful, beautiful darkness to flow into the world.

All he needed was a little more time, time that he would have when the accursed Spark was finally in his possession.

The Dreaming would be defeated.

And darkness would reign once again.

"Where are you, my little betrayer?" the Nacht asked the wall.

The Dragon brought the sphere of Dreaming up close to his face and gave it a violent shake. The First Folk wailed in terror.

"Your people cry out for you," the Nacht growled. "Do not force my hand. Do not force me to do something . . . irreversible." The Nacht sunk his razor-sharp claws into the wall, tearing some of it away.

"Bring me what I've asked you to, and all will be forgiven."

Abbey Bone thought she knew all about heroes. She knew about the kinds that were in the books she liked to read, and she knew of real ones like the three Bone cousins, her parents, and even Uncle Percival. Yep, she thought that she knew everything there was to know about these brave individuals.

But that was before she'd met the Veni Yan named Randolf.

There was something about the man, something that made her feel safe and protected, that everything was going to turn out all right.

Even when it looked like it wasn't.

They had run like crazy across the cave to find Barclay and to help the poor people being attacked by more of the awful bat beasts. And here they were, all standing together. She was even holding Barclay's hand. Though she probably wouldn't admit it, getting to be with her twin again was worth everything they had gone through.

But she had to wonder, as she looked up at the hundreds of bats swarming above them, if their reunion was going to be short lived.

And she started to be afraid — really, really afraid — until she glanced over at Randolf, who was standing with his sword in hand. And he didn't look afraid at all. He looked like he was thinking of a way to save them, and that's what got her to thinking about heroes and how Randolf was one of the special ones.

A hero's hero. That would be the way to describe him.

And knowing that he was there with them, despite how horrible it all seemed, Abbey wasn't all that scared anymore.

The Veni Yan's eyes darted about the cavern. He knew it wouldn't be long before the bats grew brave and fully descended on them in numbers too large to count.

Randolf looked over at Roque Ja. Even the great cat cringed beneath the bats, reaching up occasionally to pluck one from the air and tear it apart, but it mattered very little.

If they were going to survive, they had to get out of these caves.

"Do you have any information, anything at all that could help us escape these caves?" Randolf asked the young woman who Barclay had said was Gerta, the daughter of a Pawan Chief. The girl was tensed and holding a jagged piece of rock.

"I was always forbidden by my father to enter these mountains," Gerta said. "But that doesn't mean that I didn't explore them from time to time without his knowing."

A bat came incredibly close and attempted to pluck Randolf from the ground, but the Veni Yan swung his sword, cutting off a wing, and was aided by Gerta, who smashed her rock into its twisted face.

"The mountains are honeycombed with natural passages," the girl explained. "Most of them lead to the surface. If we could get to one of them . . . any of them, we could make our escape."

"And what of the bats?" Randolf asked.

"The tunnels are small and cramped. The bats wouldn't be able to fly within them, which takes away their advantage."

"And do you see one of these narrow passages?" Randolf asked as the bat monsters got even closer. There wasn't much time left.

"There," Gerta said, eyes squinting in the dimness of

the cave. "I think I see one there." Randolf saw where she was pointing and agreed.

"If we're going to do this it must be now." He squatted down to address the Bone twins and Roderick. "Gerta has identified an exit from this cavern," Randolf explained. "I want you all to lead the others as fast as you can toward that opening."

"And what about you?" Abbey asked.

"Yeah, what are you doing?" Barclay wanted to know.

"I'm going to provide a distraction," Randolf said. "Roque Ja and I will lead the bats away, hopefully giving you enough time to escape."

"Does Roque Ja know this?" Abbey asked, leaning over to see the great cat angrily swatting at the bats that dove at him.

"He will," Randolf said, glancing briefly at the cat. "Are you ready?"

Gerta, the twins, and Roderick nodded nervously.

"Be ready to run," Randolf said, turning toward where Roque Ja crouched.

"Be careful!" Abbey called out.

He turned and looked at her. "And you do the same."

"We're going to run now," Randolf told Roque Ja, climbing onto his back.

"What do you think you're doing?" the great cat roared, jumping to his feet.

"I'm trying to save our lives," Randolf said, taking

handfuls of thick fur and gripping them like reigns as he kicked the heels of his boots into Roque Ja's sides.

Too stunned to argue, the mountain cat bounded away from the group. Randolf was yelling at the top of his lungs, waving his sword arm in the air as he tried to capture the bats' attention.

Chancing a look behind him as Roque Ja ran, he saw that he was successful. Gerta, Roderick, and the twins were leading the bats' prisoners away in the opposite direction while the majority of the bats followed him and Roque Ja.

A cloud of abominable fury descending upon them.

"Bring me what I asked for, and all will be forgiven."

Lorimar heard the silky voice of the Nacht inside her head, trying to draw her to his realm of darkness.

Following Tom and the little Dragon down the winding stone passage, she stumbled a bit, using the wall of the tunnel to steady her mossy form.

"Are you all right, Lorimar?" Tom asked.

His body had ceased to glow, but she could see that he was still imbued with the power of the Spark. There was a light in the boy's eyes now.

"I'm fine, Tom," she told him. "Some rocks underfoot caused me to lose balance."

Tom seemed to be satisfied with her answer and faced front once again.

"I think we're on the right track," he said, continuing to lead them on.

He could sense it within the mountain, the Nacht's presence growing larger by the second. The light inside him was drawing him to it. He really had no idea of what he was supposed to do when he got there, but was sure that the Dreaming would help him in some way.

Lorimar followed the boy and the Dragon, the urgings of the Nacht and the fearful screams of her people echoing in her mind. The shadow Dragon was going to hurt them — the last of her kind — unless she gave him what he most desired.

She really had no choice.

The darkness called to him.

It was almost as if the evil had a voice, and it was singing out his name, taunting him to destroy it.

Tom couldn't have thought of a better idea.

The sounds of the bats were getting louder the closer they got, and Tom prepared himself for what he might find. Finally, up ahead he saw an opening that was illuminated in patches of glowing moss, and he was sure that on the other side of it was the evil that he was destined to face.

"This is it," Tom said, hesitating only a second before surging ahead and passing through the opening.

The air was filled with the monster bats, and it took a

moment for him to take it all in, to truly understand what he was seeing. The bats were swarming, chasing a group that was running toward them at a vicious clip.

Tom went to them, and a feeling like no other passed through him when he saw Barclay and Gerta in a furious run, with Abbey and Roderick behind them. It wasn't long before they saw him, too.

"Tom!" Barclay screamed, waving his arms.

But Tom's happiness was short lived as the living cloud of monster bats was nearly upon them.

"We have to do something," Tom said, running ahead, but then he felt a strong hand grip his arm.

He turned to look into the green and luminescent face of Lorimar, who simply said, "No."

Tom couldn't believe what he was hearing and roughly pulled his arm away. He turned back to his friends, just in time to see the little orange Dragon soaring through the air toward them.

Stillman unleashed an enormous plume of Dragon fire. The flames engulfed the attacking bats while his friends fell to the ground, staring up in awe.

The fire didn't burn the bats, but transformed them back into what they had been before the Nacht's evil touch. The monstrous creatures became the reasonably harmless cave dwellers they had once been.

Tom ran to join his friends, but was met halfway by the twins and Roderick, who were in a panic.

"What's wrong?" Tom asked.

"It's Randolf," Abbey said, pointing to the far end of the cavern. "He and Roque Ja distracted most of the bat things so that we could get away."

Tom looked to where the little Bone was pointing and saw another, much larger swarm of bats attacking something in the distance.

"Tom!" Lorimar called out, and he gave her a look before running toward the scene up ahead.

"This isn't the fight you should be concerning yourself with!" Lorimar called after him.

"I have the power inside me," Tom yelled as he ran. "If I can't use it to help my friends, what's the sense in having it?"

Stillman soared through the air ahead of him, spurring him to run faster.

Tom could see the Veni Yan through the shifting cloud of wings and black fur up ahead and what appeared to be a giant cat fighting the monsters beside the warrior. He hoped he wasn't too late.

He was so focused on Randolf that the attack took him totally by surprise. It came from somewhere inside his skull, and Tom went down on his hands and knees. He fought to stand, but he couldn't.

Kneeling in the cave, he felt his attention drawn to the enormous wall of rocks to his left. Tom sensed something behind it, something hungrily reaching out to him. He tried to ignore it — he had to get to Randolf — but the force behind the wall would have nothing of it.

And then he heard her voice, and found himself very confused.

"Don't fight it, Tom," Lorimar said, her glowing body of moss slinking from the shadows cast by the wall.

"Lorimar, what . . . ?" It was difficult to speak as she approached.

"Don't fight it, Tom," she said again, kneeling beside him. "This is how it is supposed to be."

He couldn't focus his eyes, the threat of sleep pulling at him. It was as if he was caught in a powerful current, his entire body being sucked down. And no matter how hard he fought, it wasn't enough.

"Go to him, Tom," Lorimar said, reaching out a mossy hand to caress his brow. "He wants you badly.

"And who am I to deny him?"

Chapter 17

Stillman wasn't sure how much fire he had left, but it didn't stop him from giving it his all.

The little Dragon glided toward the attacking bats, unleashing another powerful blast of purifying Dragon's flame. He tried to keep the fire going for as long as he could, watching for the occasional stray bat that attempted to flee.

He got those as well.

Now that the cloud of attacking bat monsters had been cleared, the Dragon could see what had been the object of their fury: a Veni Yan priest and the biggest mountain cat Stillman had ever seen.

The Dragon touched down, going to them both. The priest lay on the ground, his clothing torn and bloody. The great cat was also pretty ripped up, its fur matted with blood. The bodies of hundreds of dead bats lay all around them.

"Are you all right?" Stillman asked them.

The mountain cat licked one of its large paws, staring down at the unmoving man, its yellow eyes going to Stillman briefly before returning to the Veni Yan.

"I'll heal," the cat said, his voice a throaty rumble.

"And the priest?" Stillman asked, coming closer.

"It's up to him," the cat said as he stood up and walked away.

Chief Gnod stood at the outskirts of his village, gazing up at the mountains, and felt the sharp stabbing pain of shame. It couldn't have hurt worse if a sword had been run through his heart.

His daughter, his only child, had been taken up there, and he wasn't brave enough — man enough — to do anything about it, but a mere boy was. Tom Elm had gone off into the mountains to save his Bone friend, as well as Gnod's daughter, while the Chief remained at home, tormented by his fear. He had shamed not only his ancestors, but also all the Chieftains who had come before him.

Feeling as if he were no longer alone, Gnod turned to see his wife and two hounds standing there.

"Leave me to my misery, woman," Gnod commanded with a wave of his hand.

"I will do no such thing," she retorted.

Gnod glared at her. The dogs sensed their master's

disapproval and cowered by their mistress's side, refusing to look at him.

"I have watched you suffer enough," his wife said defiantly, striding closer.

The old Chief chuckled sadly. "And when I feel that I have suffered enough, the powers that be still find more ways to torment me and my people."

"And I say we give them nothing more," she said, standing very close to him. "They have taken enough. Now is the time to start taking back."

"I am empty, my wife," Gnod said. "A mere shadow of my former self. I have nothing else with which to fight."

The Chieftain's wife reached out and grabbed her husband's arm in a surprisingly powerful grip.

"Then now it is time to fill that empty vessel up again," she said forcefully. "You will do this by helping to bring my daughter back to me and to her father, the great Chief Gnod . . . and to her village."

Gnod looked to the cold mountains and then to his beloved wife of many years. "Do I dare hope that I am capable of such a task?" he asked her, feeling something writhing in his chest that he had not felt for so very long.

"Dare to hope, my beloved . . . my Chief," she said, leaning in to kiss his weathered cheek. "For without it, you have already lost."

. . .

It was as the Spark's vision had shown him: Lorimar carrying him toward a wall of rock and darkness. He tried to speak to her, to ask her what she was doing, but she ignored his questions.

The two of them passed through the wall, crossing over into a realm of shadow.

Tom dropped to his knees, nearly overcome with the most debilitating sense of fatigue. There was nothing he wanted more than to close his eyes and drift off to sleep. But something deep inside said that would be the end of him, and so much more.

The end of the world.

"Where are we?" he asked drowsily, eyes attempting to adjust to this place of shifting blackness.

"A place once filled with light and life," Lorimar said. "But now . . ."

Tom looked over to see that his friend no longer wore her mossy form or anything solid. She looked to be nothing more than a fine mist that glowed with an eerie inner light — the only light that shone in this cold, black place.

And then something moved in the shadows directly before them, something huge and frightening that could not really be seen until it opened its eyes.

Two burning circles of light beamed down at him, like the open doors of a furnace — only this fire was strangely cold.

"I didn't think you were coming," the Nacht purred.

The great Dragon of darkness showed himself, and he was far more horrifying than Tom could have imagined. The ancient reptile was huge, his body adorned in a multitude of individual scales, armor forged from the blackness of nightmare.

This is it! Tom thought, energy and anticipation rising up in him. *This is what this entire quest has been leading up to.* The power of the Spark fluttered wildly inside his chest, like frightened doves trapped inside a cage. "Get behind me, Lorimar," the boy commanded, but the ghostly form of his friend drifted past him.

"Lorimar!" Tom cried out, reaching for her, but his hands couldn't take hold of anything.

"Things take time, great Dragon," Lorimar said.

Tom didn't understand why his friend was speaking to their enemy. It was almost as if . . .

"And do you have it?" the Dragon asked, Lorimar's light illuminating his body.

Tom stared in awe of his sleek and deadly form. He was the personification of all nightmares, terror given form.

But why is Lorimar talking to him? And why hasn't he struck her down?

"I do not," Lorimar said.

The Nacht reared back with a deafening roar, spreading his wings of eternal night and bellowing to the endless darkness all about them.

"What? You dare defy me?"

"You misunderstand, Lord of Shadow," she quickly explained. "I, personally, do not have what you seek, but I have brought it to you."

Randolf sat in his favorite chair before a roaring fire, sharpening his sword. It was a simple task, one made all the more pleasurable by the location in which he did it.

He ran the whetstone across the blade's edge in one smooth stroke, thinking about how much he had missed his home.

Something gnawed at the warrior, something Randolf didn't want to think about, concentrating only on the perfect edge of his weapon.

Then there was a knock at the door.

The sharpening stone stopped midstroke. *Who could be knocking on my door at this late hour?* he wondered, panic creeping over him.

But he stamped it down. There was nothing — or nobody — at the door that he would allow himself to be concerned with. He was in his home with his family and . . .

The knock came again, this time a little more forcefully.

"Aren't you going to answer?" his wife asked from the doorway to their bedroom. She was holding a candle to light her way in the dark.

"It's nobody," he said, focusing on his sword. "Go back to bed and I'll be along shortly."

His wife didn't move, staring at the door as another knock came.

"Randolf . . ." she began.

"Please," he beckoned to her. "We don't need to answer."

His daughter emerged in her dressing gown, the little girl looking like a ghost as she flowed across the room.

"Who's at the door, Father?" she asked.

He wanted to tell her to go back to her room, that she and her mother didn't need to know, and if they ignored the knocking, whoever it was would go away.

"You're not supposed to be here with us, are you, Daddy?" she asked, her words like a crashing blow to his stomach.

"Of course I am," he said, leaning his blade against the stone of the fireplace. "I've finished my mission, and now I'm here with you. . . ." He looked over to his wife. "With both of you."

The knock came again, even more insistent this time.

"You need to answer that," his wife told him.

Randolf shook his head, feeling an overwhelming sadness pass over him. He knew that she was right.

His daughter slipped her delicate hand into his. "Come along, Father," she said, her voice like sunshine. "We'll answer together."

Randolf allowed himself to be led from the warmth of the fireplace as another knock filled the solitude of his home. He stopped momentarily, turning back to the fireplace for his sword.

"I'm likely to need this," he said, scooping up his sharpened sword and then taking his daughter's hand once more.

He stood before the door. He didn't want to leave, didn't want to give this up.

"We'll see you soon," his wife said with the loveliest of smiles.

He returned the expression, only looking much sadder.

"And how long is that?" he asked. "How long is soon?"

"When your job is done," she answered. "No more than that, or less."

And he knew that she was right, for she was always right and took great pleasure in proving this.

He squatted in front of his daughter, looking deeply into her eyes. "Promise that you'll keep the fire going for me," he told her.

"I will," his daughter said, throwing her tiny arms around his neck and hugging him close. "We'll both be here, Mommy and I, waiting for your return."

Randolf stood, knowing now in his heart that they were right, that it was not yet time for him to be here, no matter how much he desired it. There was still much to be done on the other side to keep the Valley safe.

The knock came again, and he reached for the latch to open it.

"I'm coming," he said, pulling the door open to reveal the strangest of sights.

A tiny Dragon was there and he beckoned to him to wake up.

And who was he to refuse the request of a Dragon?

Randolf opened his eyes, looking up into the Dragon's face.

"I think we might have a problem," the orange creature said.

"You . . . you're a Dragon," the Veni Yan priest said, taken aback.

"That's right. I'm Stillman, and I think Tom might be in trouble."

"Tom?" Randolf questioned, urging the confusion from his brain and pushing the memory of his wife and child to the background. "Tom's in trouble?" He sat up quickly, climbing to his feet and looking about the cave. "And the bats?"

"I took care of most of them," the Dragon said. He took the warrior priest's hand and led him over to the wall of stone.

"Where is he?" Randolf asked. "Where's Tom?"

"That's the problem," the Dragon said. "I saw him over here with the moss lady, but when I looked back they were gone."

An icy claw of dread clutched at the warrior's heart.

"I think he's behind this wall," Stillman said.

The wall began to tremble and shake, wisps of living darkness crawling out freely from between the stones.

"And I'm not sure if that's a very good place to be."

Lorimar saw the look in the boy's eyes, that moment when he realized that she had betrayed him and their quest, and she wanted so desperately to explain.

When the Nacht had presented her with the sphere and showed her that she was no longer alone, that a piece of the untouched Dreaming still existed . . . she had been blinded by pure emotion and selfishness, and would likely have promised the monster anything.

But after finding out that Tom was the missing piece of the puzzle, the remaining piece of the Spark . . .

Now she could truly see.

Lorimar saw that nothing mattered, that she had to do exactly as the shadow Dragon wanted. She needed to deliver the Spark to him.

The Dragon lowered himself menacingly toward her, plucking the orb from beneath his wing and taunting her with it. Tom saw that within the orb was the most beautiful of forests and was reminded of what he had seen in his dreams — of his memories of the Dreaming.

"The boy . . . he has it?" the Nacht asked.

"He does," Lorimar answered. She could feel Tom's eyes on her, but she refused to look.

"Lorimar, what are you doing?" he begged, but she ignored his pleas.

"The boy has the Spark," she told the Nacht. "And all you need do is take it."

The Dragon turned his burning eyes to the boy. "That shouldn't be too difficult," he grumbled.

Lorimar stepped toward the fearsome beast. "But first there is the matter of the sphere," she said, pointing to the transparent globe the monster still held.

"Of course," the Nacht said, pulling the sphere closer. "The Spark first, and then you shall have the sphere."

She tried to catch her peoples' attention, reassuring them with a smile and a nod, before turning back to Tom. The evil spirits of the place were holding him, preventing him from running away. But then again, where would he go?

Her gaze met his, and this time she tried to make him understand.

"Don't be afraid, Tom," she called to him. "Give the great and powerful Nacht what he desires."

The Dragon reached down with a claw, snatching up the boy and lifting him from the ground.

"Listen to your friend, boy," the shadow Dragon said.

"She's no friend!" Tom wailed, struggling in the monster's grasp as he glared at her accusingly.

"Give me the Spark and perhaps I'll be merciful and allow you to join your family in eternal slumber."

"Give it to him, Tom," Lorimar called. "Show him the true power of what he desires."

A mere moment ago, Tom had never hated anyone more, but suddenly, in a passing blink, he understood what was happening. There was a look from the ghostly woman, a hint of something in her eyes.

"Give it to me!" the Nacht roared, the stink of his breath reminding Tom of every bad thing he'd experienced in his twelve years of life.

"Give me the Spark!" the demon of shadow bellowed, shaking his body like one of his sister's rag dolls.

Lottie.

Tom's mind quickly traveled to thoughts of his family and of all the others who were held in the spell of the Nacht's growing evil. He looked out over the monster's realm of shadow, horrified that the rolling landscape was actually the sleeping forms of all those who had fallen to the Nacht's touch.

So far.

It was a frightening sight to behold, and he imagined his family out there among countless others.

But aside from the fear, there was anger, a fire growing

inside of him. A light that had been preserved since the beginning for a time such as this.

"Do not make me hurt you, boy," the great Dragon threatened. "I would think nothing of plucking off your arms and legs to get what I want." The Nacht glowered at him, bringing him closer. "Or perhaps I will sift through the many sleeping to find your loved ones and make them pay for your insolence. Would you dare me to do that, Tom Elm, leader of the quest?"

The monster was mocking him and his brave friends, and he knew that now was the time to give the monster exactly what he was asking for.

"Please," he begged. "Do not harm my family, or anyone else for that matter. I will give you what you want."

The Dragon smiled, showing off rows of sharp teeth that glistened in the dim light like freshly unearthed coal.

"I knew you could be reasonable," the Nacht growled, watching him with his horrible, burning eyes.

Tom slowly reached inside his tunic for something that was no longer there, but the Dragon did not know this.

"Here," Tom said, holding out a closed hand.

The Dragon came closer, sniffing at Tom's fist as he turned it around, then opened his fingers to reveal nothing.

"What?" the Dragon bellowed as he grabbed Tom's wrist. "You wish to play games with me?"

"No games," Tom said as he shook his head, summoning the light within his very being. "You wanted the Spark?"

Tom's body began to glow brighter and brighter, and the Dragon screamed in outrage and pain, but was too stupid and stubborn to release the boy.

"Here I am," Tom said, his body pulsing with the intensifying power.

"No!" the Dragon wailed. "I was so close . . . I was —"

"Take me . . ."

The Nacht tried to throw him away, but it was too late. The light blazed fully, its brilliance pushing back the darkness and shadow that had taken hold of the Dreaming.

"I am the light."

The Nacht tried to escape the light of the Spark, but it was too fast and too bright. The light attacked hungrily, refusing to let him get away. Little by little the burning radiance fed upon the darkness that made him the terror that he was. The Nacht tried to fight it, but the Spark's power continued to intensify, dwarfing his own.

The Spark had become all things, filling every nook and cranny of the Dreaming, washing away the darkness in a deluge of brilliance.

As his body disintegrated, the Nacht knew his time was over, and turned his hateful gaze to the boy who was the light.

The boy who was the Spark.

The boy who was his end.

Gran'ma Ben suddenly came awake with a loud gasp, the light of the sun shining in her eyes. She sat up and looked around, and saw that she had been lying in the gateway to the city.

Where she had fallen as she was trying to leave the Kingdom to get help.

Her horse was already up and around, nibbling at some stray tufts of grass growing just outside Atheia's gates. Things were slowly coming into focus for the old woman, as if she were being pulled from some thick mud where she had been trapped for . . .

Gran'ma Ben had no idea how long she'd been unconscious.

She got to her feet, suddenly remembering the most important thing of all, and started to run for the castle. As she ran, she saw that others were starting to come awake, too.

Gran'ma Ben wasn't quite sure what had happened, but she knew that it had been terrible, and whatever it was had affected the entire Valley. Flashes of darkness appeared before her mind's eye, and in the darkness, something huge and powerful sat, like a big fat spider in the center of a web, all those touched by its evil spread out before it. An icy chill raced up and down her spine.

The newly awakened cried out to her as she passed, wanting to know what had befallen them, but she kept on running, not knowing enough herself to shed any light on . . .

That was it. There had been a flash of light somewhere in the deep, dank dark, and it had been so warm and filled with life.

And in that light there had been a boy, and somehow she knew that this boy was special and that he had risked everything to bring the light and chase away the darkness.

It was coming to her, in drips and drabs, the enormity of it all becoming clearer, and all the more frightening.

Gran'ma Ben was in the castle now and ran down the corridor, pushing herself as if this were the most important of all cow races.

She had to be sure. She had to be sure that she was safe.

The heavy wooden door to the room was already partially open, and the old woman slammed into it with enough force to send it flying back, crashing into the wall.

Gran'ma Ben's eyes immediately went to the bed, fearing that she would find her granddaughter still held tightly in the grip of unnatural sleep.

But the bed was empty.

"Thorn!" Grand'ma Ben bellowed.

"Gran'ma," said a soft voice still weak from sleep, and she spun around to find the Queen standing in front of the

open window, bathed in a swath of radiant sunshine.

"Are you all right, girl?" Gran'ma Ben asked, going to her granddaughter and taking her in her arms.

"I'm fine now," Thorn said dreamily, and Gran'ma Ben wondered how much Thorn could remember.

"He saved us," Thorn said to her.

"Who?" Gran'ma asked, but then knew the answer.

"The boy. The boy who carried the Spark. He saved us all."

CHAPTER 18

He had walked from one side of the great stone wall to the other, searching for signs of the boy.

"Are you sure you saw him over here?" the Veni Yan priest asked the Dragon.

Just as Stillman was about to answer, the wall began to shake. It had already been trembling and rumbling, but nothing like this. Randolf jumped away from the wall as giant pieces of stone began to crash down, beams of pure, white light cutting through the spaces between the rocks that comprised the barrier.

"What's happening?" Randolf asked as he joined the Dragon's side.

Rays of light continued to stream from the cracks in the quaking wall and fill the darkened chamber, turning night into day. Randolf watched as the Dragon cautiously approached the wall.

"Careful, Dragon," the Veni Yan priest urged.

But Stillman did not appear to be listening and stood directly before a section of the great barrier. The light touched the Dragon, illuminating his entire body, and Randolf saw a strange expression cross Stillman's face.

"This is something wonderful," the tiny Dragon said.

But then there was a rumble, and Randolf watched as a section of the great wall crumbled, an avalanche of rock tumbling down to where the Dragon was standing. The Veni Yan dove at the Dragon and knocked him from the path of falling stone.

The air was filled with the dust of pulverized rock, and Randolf and Stillman both coughed.

"Thanks," Stillman said, waving a hand before his face to clear the air.

Randolf climbed to his feet, his eyes fixed to the spot where the rocks had fallen, fixed to a passage from which a blinding light emanated. Something moved in the light, a dark outline coming through from the other side. Randolf tensed, seeking his sword as he got between the Dragon and whatever was coming.

He breathed a sigh of relief when he saw that it was the quest's leader.

"Tom," Randolf said, feeling happier than he'd felt in a long time.

Tom smiled as he walked across the fallen rocks. "We

won," he said, stopping to look back into the light from which he'd come. "And it's beautiful."

Before Randolf could ask the boy what had occurred and where he had been, Tom tumbled forward in a lifeless heap, unconscious.

And then what remained of the wall *really* began to shake.

Percival brought the *Queen of the Sky* around once more, spinning the wheel with expert precision as they all searched for signs of life.

"Anything?" he called out from the wheelhouse. He had them all looking — the Constable and his men on one side, the two Rats on the other.

"Nothing yet!" one of the deputies cried out.

"I don't see anything either," said the little turtle who was kneeling atop the *Queen*'s control board, face pressed against the cracked glass of the wheelhouse. "But my eyesight isn't what it used to be."

"That's okay," Percival said, looking out through the windows as well, scanning the mountain crags below. "You just give a shout if you think you see anything at all."

Porter turned to look at him. "Do you think he's all right?"

Percival's thoughts went to multiple places: to Barclay and Abbey, to Tom, and then to Randolf, Lorimar, and Roderick.

The turtle must have seen the concern in his expression.

"I was talking about Stillman," Porter said. "But I bet you were thinking about your friends."

"That I was," Percival said. "That I was."

"Down there!" Stinky suddenly wailed.

"What is it?" Percival yelled from the doorway of the wheelhouse. "What do you see?"

"The two Bone desserts," Stinky said, and was savagely elbowed by his partner.

"I mean children," the Rat corrected. "The two Bone children and a gaggle of humans coming from a cave below!"

Percival felt as though his heart might burst, steering the front of the *Queen* around so that he could see. The Rats were right. Down below, emerging from a cave in the mountain were Abbey and Barclay, as well as quite a few other folks. Percival wasn't sure if he'd ever experienced such relief before, seeing the twins alive and relatively safe. . . .

But something was happening to the mountain.

At first he thought it might be the rumble of an approaching storm, but then he could see the mountain actually tremble, and suddenly bright light shone from every crack, cleft, and fissure.

Percival immediately put his makeshift crew to work.

"Get the rope ladder over the side," he ordered. "We gotta get them off that mountain as quickly as possible."

"What's happening?" Porter asked, his little turtle

eyes practically bugging from his head as he gazed at the shaking mountain below.

"I think that mountain is coming down."

The chamber was collapsing. A storm of rock and choking dust rained down on Tom, Randolf, and Stillman as they attempted to escape the vast cavern. Flashes of brilliance from beyond the great wall lit their way, illuminating the openings in the underground cavity.

Randolf paused momentarily to shift the still-unconscious Tom on his shoulders and to make sure that the little Dragon had not been lost.

"Quickly now," he said. "I see a passage up ahead that's still open."

There was a great distance they still had to manage, but they had no choice — it was either take the chance, or be buried alive. Without another word, they ran. Huge boulders rained down from the ceiling, smashing to earth all around them. Stillman, being smaller and faster, had gone ahead, guiding them across the treacherous expanse.

"Almost there, Tom," Randolf said to the boy who could not hear him.

They were no more then twenty feet away when the unthinkable happened. The cave floor seemed to shift suddenly, groaning like an old man rising from his bed, and an avalanche of huge pieces of broken stone poured down to block their escape route.

All Randolf could do was stare.

"We'll never move these in time," Stillman said, pulling away some of the stones, but there were too many.

Randolf was already searching for another way out, his keen eyes trying to pierce the thick clouds of dust. He wasn't about to give up, especially after all they'd been through. They had come too far for it to end this way.

Something moved through the dust to his left, and suddenly the giant mountain cat stood before him.

"I thought you'd left," Randolf said, shifting Tom's weight on his back.

Roque Ja turned his yellow eyes to their obstructed escape route. "Move," the great cat growled to Stillman, who did as he was told.

Roque Ja pounced on the broken rocks as if they were prey, swipes of his mighty paws moving rubble aside that would have taken them hours to deal with.

The strange, searing light was flashing brighter now, each new blinding explosion bringing more upheaval to the chamber. It wouldn't be long before the whole thing came down.

Above the din of falling rock and rubble, Randolf heard the clearing of a massive throat and returned his attention to Roque Ja, who was about to enter the newly cleared passage.

"Coming?" the great cat asked with a swish of his tail.

Randolf and Stillman darted for the opening as more of the chamber fell down behind them.

They didn't need to be asked twice.

The ground rolled beneath Chief Gnod's feet. The leader of the Pawa swiftly raised his hand, halting his hunting party, and gazed up to the mountains on the path ahead.

It was almost as if the mountain was warning him, telling him to stay away, to accept his people's — and daughter's — fate.

But the Chief had had enough. He and his clan had paid for their sins, and it was time for them to start living again.

Squinting his old eyes, he could see clouds billowing up in the distance, followed by the roll of what sounded like thunder.

"The mountains are angry," one of the hunting party said.

Gnod turned to look at him, a young man by the name of Brand. He was one of the braver of the village and perhaps someone who might someday be Chief.

But not yet.

The youth's eyes, as well as those of the other six in their party, were filled with fear.

"And I'm angry, too," Chief Gnod responded. "Angry that we've come to this . . . brave men cowering in the shadows as our people were taken in the night . . . angry that we allowed a mere boy to go up into those mountains alone to rescue one of our own . . . angry that it has taken me this long to remember that I am Chieftain of this clan and that I have a responsibility to each and every one of you . . ."

Gnod looked back up into the mountains.

". . . and them. And I don't care if the mountains are angry or not."

He turned back to the hunting party, trying to instill in each and every one of them the hope and courage that he had found, and one at a time he saw it appear, the spark of something that hadn't been there for a long time.

"Let us go and see what our mountains are so angry about," the Chieftain said, turning back onto the trail that would take them higher.

And the hunting party followed their Chief without hesitation.

Percival brought the *Queen of the Sky* to hover as close to the crumbling mountain as he was able, and one by one they brought the folks that had come from the cave aboard, most of them filthy and exhausted. Percival wondered what had gone on inside the mountain, positive that it had to do with the Nacht and his plans for the Valley.

Percival was eager to get Abbey, Barclay, and Roderick aboard to fill him in on what he missed, but the kids, proving once again that they had the hearts of true adventurers, were making sure that the others in worse shape than themselves were able to climb aboard the *Queen* first.

When the last of the folks from the cave were safe and sound, finally the twins, their raccoon friend, and a pretty girl were on their way up the ladder.

"Well, you're certainly a sight for sore eyes," Percival said as Abbey climbed over the side and ran into her uncle's arms. Barclay followed right behind her to get in on some of the hugging action as well.

"We sure did miss you, Unc," Abbey said, squeezing him with all her might.

"We weren't even sure if you and the *Queen* had made it," Barclay said.

Roderick had scampered up and was now perched precariously on Percival's shoulder, kissing his head.

"Never count your old uncle or the *Queen of the Sky* out, kids," Percival said, and was nearly overcome with emotion as he held his family close, for he had feared that he would never get to hold his niece and nephew in his arms again.

Percival then noticed that the pretty young girl was standing at the side of the *Queen*, looking over at the mountains below.

"Who's your friend?" he asked the kids.

"She's Barclay's friend. I just met her running like crazy from the caves," Abbey said.

"Her name's Gerta," Barclay said. "Her father's a Pawa Chief or something. I think she's worried about Tom."

"Tom?" Percival said. "Is he all right?"

Barclay shrugged. "I don't know. He and Lorimar showed up with a little Dragon and saved us from the bat creatures."

"Bat creatures?" Percival asked, wondering if they were what had caused the *Queen* to crash.

Barclay nodded vigorously. "And then they went to help Randolf and Roque Ja."

Stinky and Smelly screamed at the mention of the giant cat and ran to hide beneath a nearby tarp.

"And what happened after that?" Percival was desperate to know, going over to the side to stand beside Gerta and look down on the mountain.

"We don't know," Gerta said sadly. "The cave started to come down, and we needed to get my people to safety."

"So we don't know if Tom, and the others . . ."

Percival didn't finish his sentence, the quiet that now filled the deck of the *Queen* providing more than words.

CHAPTER 19

In the light of the Spark, Tom saw them all awaken. Each and every one who had been taken by the darkness of the Nacht was awake again.

"And it's all because of you, Tom," Lorimar said weakly.

Tom found himself standing in a glade of young green, the vegetation all around him in the earliest stages of healthy growth. The Dreaming was shucking off the shock of darkness and was growing again.

Lorimar stood beneath the drooping bow of a great tree, her ghostly form even more vague than before. It was almost as if she were fading away.

"I can barely see you," Tom said.

"Soon there will be nothing of me to see," she said.

Tom felt a moment of panic, watching as Lorimar became even more indistinct. "I don't understand," he said. "We won . . . the Dreaming . . ."

"The Dreaming is safe once more because of you."

Tom noticed movement close by and was surprised to see more of Lorimar's kind — more of the First Folk — coming toward them.

"I thought you were the last?" he said.

"As did I," Lorimar answered in the faintest of whispers. "But the Nacht had saved a piece of my world and offered it to me in exchange for the Spark. He wanted me to betray you and the quest."

"I thought that you had," Tom told her.

"And I apologize for that deception," she said. "But I would be lying to you if I said that I did not consider the black Dragon's offer." She stared past him out at the Dreaming as it healed. "But when I saw that you were the missing piece . . . that you were the living embodiment of the Spark . . ."

She looked at him with eyes that were filled with life and hope.

"I knew that I must risk everything to see the quest succeed."

"And it has," Tom said.

"The sphere used to tempt me acted as a seed, and, along with the Spark, helped the Dreaming to begin to restore herself to her former glory."

Tom looked around at the new life. "It looks as though she's off to a good start," he said.

"And it is all thanks to you," Lorimar said.

Tom shook his head. "It wasn't just me," he explained. "It was all of us . . . Randolf, Percival and the twins, you and Roderick, Stillman the Dragon . . . and even the Rats. We could never have come this far without them all."

"You were the Spark," Lorimar began, "and we the rays that came from your brilliance. One could not exist without the other."

Tom liked the comparison and smiled. "Yeah, that sounds about right," he said.

They had started to walk now, crossing the fields of growing grass.

"So what now?" Tom asked.

"Now the Dreaming continues to heal and grow."

"And me and the others?"

"You all go back to your lives," Lorimar said. "The Dreaming, the Valley, and even the vast world beyond will be forever in your debt."

Tom was looking at her again, her shape even less distinct than it had been before.

"And you?"

"The Nacht's dark magic was strong," she said. "It took everything that I had to shatter the sphere that imprisoned my brethren." Lorimar turned her ghostly form to her kind. "I am but a dwindling flame now," she said. "What remains of me will be joined to them."

"Are you . . ." Tom began. "Are you going to die?"

Lorimar drifted closer to her people, and they encircled her fading form.

"As long as the spark of memory remains . . ." she said, what was left of her body becoming like smoke and flowing into the bodies of her people.

"*I live.*"

The moss covering the large boulder first began to smolder, and then large cracks zigzagged across its craggy surface before it exploded into thousands of much smaller pieces of rock, exposing the long tunnel passage that led to daylight.

Stillman stumbled from the opening, mouth smoking. He didn't think he'd ever been so tired and wanted nothing more than to return to his little cave at the bottom of the forest lake and sleep.

A quick fifty-year nap would do him just fine.

"We made it," the little Dragon said between pants. He turned to his new friend, motioning with his little hands to follow. "C'mon, you can do it."

The Veni Yan came first, the boy still unconscious and draped over his shoulders, followed by the mountain cat Roque Ja. They were all exhausted from running for their lives, but at least they'd made it.

And just in the nick of time because Stillman knew that he didn't have any more to give, that the last burst of fire he'd breathed to free them from the passage was it for him. He could no longer feel the fire churning, hot and special in his belly. It was gone — all used up. And as he sat on a piece of shattered boulder to rest, he was grateful that there had been enough.

"That's it," Stillman said. "I'm done with the running and the saving for a little while."

Randolf sat down, too, wiping dust and dirt from his sweating face while Roque Ja curled up and immediately began snoring.

Tom was on the ground where Randolf had laid him. His eyes flew open, and he looked around, a smile on his face as he slowly sat up.

"We made it," he said triumphantly. "We're safe."

Stillman was just about to agree when he heard it, a nasty hissing sound that could have come from only one thing. The others heard it as well, all lifting their tired heads and looking around for the source.

"You've got to be kidding me," Stillman said wearily as a pack of mangy, hungry-looking Rat Creatures emerged from hiding and began to circle them.

"See, my brothers," the leader of the Rats snarled. "I told you if we looked long enough, we would find food for our bellies."

The Rats growled, thick strings of slimy spit dribbling from their hungry mouths as they slowly advanced.

"And look at what I've found for us," the leader proclaimed. "Enough food to fill our empty stomachs . . . and to have seconds."

Stillman sensed someone beside him and looked to see that Tom was standing there.

"So," Stillman began, eyes carefully watching the approaching Rats. "Is this what it's like hanging around with you all the time?"

"Seems like it," Tom answered.

"Must be hard to keep friends."

"Yeah, but the ones I do have are very special," Tom said.

Randolf had risen to his feet and now stood on Stillman's other side.

"Evil is nothing, if not persistent," the Veni Yan priest said, again preparing for a fight.

"Roque Ja awake yet?" Stillman asked as the Rats stalked closer.

The great cat opened one eye, saw what was happening and shut it again, snoring even louder than he had been before.

"Guess that answers that," Stillman said.

"It appears we must deal with these attackers on our own," Randolf said.

"Do you think it would help if I told them that I defeated the Nacht and saved the Dreaming and the Valley?" Tom asked, tensing.

"I doubt it," Stillman said as he reached down to pick up a rock to use to defend himself. In the old days, he was pretty good with rocks.

"Didn't think so," Tom said. The Rats were so close now that they could smell their filthy animal stink.

"Brothers, we eat!" the Rat leader proclaimed. But just as he was about to pounce, something flew down from the hills above, plunging into the rocky ground and distracting the beast.

"You'll dine not upon the friends of the Pawa this day, mangy beasts," an older man with a flowing fur cape declared as more spears rained down, driving the Rat Creatures away from their prey.

"Friends of yours?" Stillman asked.

"Yeah," Tom said with a grin. "It's Chief Gnod and some of his warriors."

Stillman breathed a sigh of relief. "They couldn't have picked a better time for a visit."

The men of Pawa descended from the cliffs, corralling the filthy Rats and holding them at bay with the points of their spears and swords.

Tom watched as Chief Gnod approached, a sick feeling forming in the pit of his belly. Tom knew that he would ask about his daughter, but he didn't have the answers that the old Chief was searching for.

Gnod stopped just before him, and Tom could see

the question in the old man's eyes.

"I didn't think I would see you again," Gnod said.

"Honestly, I felt the same way when I started up into these mountains," Tom answered.

"Seeing you like this . . ." the Chief lifted a thick, weathered hand. "Seeing you before me has given me re-newed hope that . . ."

Tom was about to interrupt, wanting to let the Chief know that he had seen his daughter alive, along with the others taken from his village, but that he was unsure what had happened after the caves had started to collapse.

He never got the chance.

The cry of *monster* suddenly filled the air, and Tom and the others were immediately on alert. Even the Rats had clumped together, looking up into the sky as the men of Pawa pointed out what they thought to be some sort of sky creature.

But was, in fact, one of the happiest sights that Tom had ever seen.

"What is that . . . thing?" Gnod whispered fearfully, drawing his sword from the scabbard.

"There's no need to be afraid," Tom said, placing a hand on the Chief's sword arm. "That's my friend's sky ship," he said, shielding his eyes from the bright sun with one hand while waving with the other.

"A sky ship?" Gnod asked. "I would never have imagined . . ."

As the *Queen of the Sky* floated closer, Tom was greeted with the most amazing of sights. Not only were his friends all aboard, waving furiously, but so was the Chief's beautiful, smiling daughter and all the others who had been taken by the evil bats. The Chief gasped, followed by the raucous cheers of his men.

It was one of the most wonderful sounds Tom had ever heard.

CHAPTER 20

Though he barely knew the tiny Dragon and the turtle, Tom was sad to see them go.

"Sure we can't give you a ride?" he asked, gesturing toward the *Queen of the Sky* hovering in an area cleared for the sky vessel in the Pawan village.

"No, that's fine," Stillman said. "We could use the walk, right, Porter?"

"Speak for yourself," said the turtle. "I'm exhausted."

Tom laughed, wanting to help the little turtle out, but it appeared that Stillman had made up his mind.

"Well, thanks for everything," Tom said.

"You're not mad because I lit you on fire, are you?" Stillman asked.

"No, that's all right," Tom said, remembering the feeling of the flames as they engulfed him, igniting the piece of Spark that existed inside of him. "You did what had to be done." They stood there, staring at one another, and Tom got a sense that the Dragon wanted to leave. "I don't want to keep you," he said.

"Yeah, we really should get going," Stillman said, looking to his companion. "Shall we?"

"You're the one who has his heart set on walking," Porter said huffily.

Tom bid them good-bye a final time, watching the two tiny figures as they walked the path that led from the village until they were both out of sight.

Then he turned, heading toward the *Queen* to see how things were going with loading the supplies.

"Can you believe it?" Percival asked him as he came aboard. Percival took another basket of potatoes from one of the Pawan women, handed it to the Constable, who handed it to one of his deputies, who handed it to another deputy, who placed it alongside the seven other baskets. "We've hit the jackpot," Percival said happily.

"And we can even eat some!" Roderick said through a mouthful of potato. "There's more than enough to go around."

Barclay reached down into one of the baskets and grabbed a potato, wiping away some of the dirt. "There's more than enough here to get us back to Boneville," he said, getting ready to have a bite.

"Not if you and Roderick don't quit eating them all," Abbey said, slapping the potato from her brother's hand

and making it fall back down into the nearly overflowing basket.

"Hey!" Barclay screeched, rubbing his hand. "Did you see that, Tom?" the little Bone asked. "She hit me!"

Tom saw nothing but trouble coming from this, and turned his attention elsewhere. He crossed the deck of the *Queen*, hearing the sounds of quarrel going on behind him and the sound of Percival Bone about to lose his patience.

Stinky and Smelly were off by themselves, quietly looking out over the side of the ship at something. Stinky stroked what little remained of his squirrel as he looked out, and Tom saw that they were staring at the captive King Agak and his soldiers. The Rats had been brought back to the village and placed inside an unused goat pen, under the constant watch of Pawan soldiers.

"I wonder what will happen to them?" Stinky asked his companion.

"I hear that they're going to let them go," Tom answered as he approached them.

"Go?" Stinky questioned.

"Yeah," Tom said. "I asked Chief Gnod to go easy on them, seeing as they were probably being used by the Nacht and all. He said that he'd do it for me, but they'll receive a strict warning to never enter Pawan territory again, or next time there won't be any mercy."

The Rats were quiet.

"They'll probably be heading home," Stinky said wistfully. "Do you remember home, Smelly?" he asked.

Smelly sighed, nodding his head. The furry beast looked incredibly sad.

"So," Tom began, "since the quest is finished, and everybody will be heading back to their lives, where are you two going?"

The Rats looked at each other, a silent message passing between the pair.

From the corner of his eye, Tom saw someone waving and looked out to see Gerta approaching the *Queen* with her father. Tom again experienced that weird, fluttering sensation in his chest at the sight of her, and wondered if he might be getting sick.

He walked down the gangplank and greeted them both with a smile. "Sir," he said with a slight bow to the Chief. "Gerta."

Her cheeks flushed a rosy pink and she quickly averted her eyes from his.

"Tom," she said in the softest of voices.

"You'll be leaving us soon," Gnod said, watching as more potatoes were brought aboard under Percival and the twins' supervision.

"As soon as we load all the provisions, we'll be ready," Tom said. "I can't thank you enough for the hospitality you've shown us."

The Chief raised a hand to silence him. "You've done far more for me and my clan than I could ever explain," he said. "Never mind the fact that you and your friends helped to save this Valley from a threat far greater than we could ever imagine. It is us that owe you all a debt of gratitude."

"Your hospitality and the potatoes are gratitude enough," Tom told the Chief.

"You are of the Pawa now," Chief Gnod told him. "You and all your friends. We would be honored to have you return for a visit anytime."

Tom looked to see that Gerta was staring at him. Her eyes were a beautiful blue, so deep that he could imagine swimming in them.

What a weird thought. Maybe I am *getting sick.*

But he thought a visit to the Pawa — and Gerta — might be something he'd like to do. Who knew, maybe he could convince his father to come with him and bring some turnips.

"I'd like that very much," Tom told the Chief, and Gerta's smile got twice as big and four times as beautiful.

There was a commotion behind him, and Tom turned to see that the Rat Creatures were being released from their pen.

"As I promised," the Chief said. "Hopefully they have the intelligence not to come back."

"I again thank you for honoring my request and . . ."

Tom began, but his words were interrupted by the most unnerving of shrieks.

"Wait!" screamed one.

"Don't leave without us!" screamed another.

Tom stared in awe at the sight of Stinky and Smelly barreling down the gangplank behind him to the village below. The men of Pawa immediately reacted to the sight of two Rat Creatures coming toward them, and readied their weapons for a fight.

"No!" Tom cried, running to intervene. "They don't mean you any harm." He managed to get in front of the Rats, holding out his hands to stop them.

"What are you doing?" he asked.

"We're going home," Stinky said, looking around Tom to see the King and the solider Rats still there, who were watching the scene.

"It is time that we face up to the responsibility of what we have done," said Smelly.

Tom turned slightly to look at the Rat King. "Are you sure you want to do this?" he asked. He knew deep down that the Rat Creatures were cold-blooded and cunning monsters, but these two had somehow wormed their way into his heart, and he didn't want to see anything bad happen to them.

The Rats nodded vigorously, and Tom stepped aside, allowing the Rats to approach their King.

"Great King Agak," Smelly began.

Agak surged at them with a ferocious snarl, and the two cowered beneath his reproach.

"How dare you two speak to me!" Agak growled.

The soldier Rats snarled, growled, and spit in the pair's direction.

"We humbly apologize, great King," Smelly said, still averting his eyes. "But we must speak if we are to apologize for our sins . . ."

"And rightfully return what had been stolen from you," Stinky added. He raised his hand, presenting the King with what remained of the dead squirrel that had been named Fredrick.

"Can it be?" Agak questioned, taken aback by the offering.

There was little more than a tail remaining, and the King hesitated before plucking the offering from Stinky's hands.

"There isn't much left," the King said, sniffing at the matted gray fur. "But then again, the tail is my favorite part."

The pair cowered together, awaiting their fate, as Agak continued to appraise his offering.

Tom considered stepping up and saying a few words in the pair's defense, but realized that he'd be speaking with a monster that, along with the possessed Constable and his Deputies, had been trying to kill them. He decided to keep

his mouth shut and let destiny take its course.

"And you return my rightful property to me why?" Agak asked.

"We realized that we were wrong," Smelly said.

"And wish to return with you . . . to our home," Stinky added.

Agak continued to smell the squirrel tail, closing his large black eyes as he inhaled the fragrant aroma. Lowering the tail, he fixed Stinky and Smelly in an intense stare as he considered their request.

"If allowed to accompany us, will you ever steal from me again?" Agak asked, his gaze going from one to the other.

"Never," Smelly swore, crossing his heart.

Stinky's eyes had gone to the squirrel tail that Agak still caressed between his clawed fingers.

"Will you steal from me again?" Agak asked again, this time speaking directly to Stinky.

Again the Rat hesitated, but an elbow jab from Smelly released his answer in a loud squeak.

"Nope!"

King Agak again studied them both, then suddenly turned his back on them and stalked away on all fours to join his soldiers. Tom watched the heartbroken pair huddle together, feeling bad for them when Agak suddenly turned.

"Are you coming, or do you plan to throw my mercy back in my face?"

That was all that the two needed to hear, and they scrabbled across the ground to rejoin their brethren. Tom would have liked to say good-bye and thank them for what they had contributed to the quest, but they were Rat Creatures, and what did he expect?

Off in the distance, he saw Stinky turn and wave good-bye before he and Smelly and the others disappeared from view.

What did he expect indeed.

Randolf watched the Rats go, not feeling much of anything at their departure. There was a time not long ago when he would have felt nothing but rage in seeing the creatures set free.

But now he simply felt — nothing.

"You're leaving?" Roque Ja asked from where he perched on a rock, licking his wounds.

"We are," the Veni Yan answered.

"Good," Roque Ja answered, lifting his bulk from the rock and stretching. Randolf could hear the cat's joints pop and crack as he stuck his large rump in the air and yawned.

"Thank you for all your help," the Veni Yan said.

Roque Ja stared at the man for a moment, his yellow eyes large and penetrating.

"I helped myself," he said gruffly, turning with a swish of his tail. "You just happened to benefit from my efforts."

"Then I thank you for those efforts," Randolf said to the powerful beast as he watched him saunter away.

"Hurrumph," Roque Ja said without bothering to turn around.

Randolf just smiled, at ease with himself and the world in which he continued to live.

The journey home felt like it was taking forever. They'd already stopped once to return the Constable and his men to their village, and Tom couldn't wait until the *Queen* was flying again. Though it did make him feel good to see the village and all those who lived in it awake again and to know that he had something to do with it.

Tom gazed out over the *Queen*'s side, watching as the Valley slowly passed below him, looking for a familiar sight that would tell him that he was getting close.

But he hadn't seen it yet.

"Do you see anything?" asked Randolf, crossing the deck to stand beside him and share the view.

"Nothing yet," Tom said with a sigh.

"No?" Randolf asked, looking down through some wispy, low-hanging clouds. "But it's right there below you, how could you miss it?"

"I thought you were talking about my home," Tom said.

"I was," the Veni Yan priest answered with a smile. "The Valley is your home, and it's my home, too . . . and you saved it and very likely even the world beyond it."

Tom looked down at the passing landscape with a different eye.

"We owe you a great debt of thanks, Tom Elm," Randolf said. "For all that you've done."

"I didn't do it alone," Tom corrected him.

"True, but it was you who carried and unleashed the Spark, restoring the Dreaming to a healthy place."

"I did what I had to do," Tom said. "Like we all did."

Randolf stared at him, and he began to feel self-conscious.

"What is it?" he asked. "What are you looking at?"

"I can now see completely why the Dreaming chose you," he said. "I'll be honest — at first I couldn't believe that she had picked you, a mere boy, but . . . as the quest went on I gradually realized what she saw in you."

"What did the Dreaming see?" Tom asked, curious.

"A hero," Randolf said, reaching out to place a firm hand on Tom's shoulder. "It was something that you were born to be."

"But now, without the Spark, I'm just a boy again," Tom said, looking through the passing clouds.

"Just a boy?" Randolf said incredulously. "My friend Tom, I'm afraid that after what you've been through, your days of being just a boy are long behind you."

Tom thought about this. "Boy, hero, turnip farmer . . . whatever I am, I'm heading home to my family after being away too long." Tom then realized what he had said and quickly apologized. "I'm sorry, Randolf," he said. "I didn't mean to bring up family. . . ."

The Veni Yan stared wistfully into the distance. "That's perfectly all right, Tom," he said. "Someday I will return to my family, too, and I look forward to our eventual reunion, but for now . . ."

"What's next, Randolf?" Tom asked.

"Ah," he said, eyes twinkling, the sadness that Tom had always seen there now replaced with something akin to a fire flickering to life. "That is the question that I'm most looking forward to answering."

Tom Elm had dreamed of this very moment. He looked over the side of the sky ship and down through the trees to see his house there, waiting for him below. This was all the payment he would need for saving the Valley from darkness.

He'd imagined his return would happen exactly like this, only — strangely enough — the reality was moving much slower. But he didn't mind, and used the time to commit it all to memory, every detail that he would re-member for the rest of his life:

The angle of the sun in the sky and the way it reflected

off the shiny leaves of the oak trees that surrounded his house, the places on the roof of his house that would need repair as the winter season approached, the sound coming from the *Queen*'s balloons as Percival released some of their gas so that the sky craft could drop closer . . .

Closer . . . closer . . . closer . . .

Tom couldn't stand it anymore, running to where the rope ladder lay tangled on the deck. He took it into his arms and prepared to throw it over the side. He saw that Roderick and the twins were looking at him, and a special message passed between him and his raccoon buddy.

"We're home, Tom," Roderick said. Tom couldn't even respond, the smile on his face so big that it made his cheeks hurt. He tossed the ladder over the side and watched as it unraveled on its way to the grass below. Seeing that they were close enough, Tom swung himself over the side and began his descent. On his way down, he recalled in a flash of memory the first time he'd ever climbed up the ladder to the deck of the *Queen of the Sky*, when the quest had just begun.

On one level it seemed to have happened so very long ago, but on another, it was like only yesterday. So much had happened since that first trip up the ladder.

So much had changed.

The more he thought about it, the more he realized Randolf was right. He was no longer the same person. He couldn't wait to share the things he had seen and done with his family.

His family.

They were the reason for everything, his own personal spark that had motivated him when he'd felt like stopping. As he reached the end of the rope ladder, he hesitated briefly, then let his feet touch the ground.

What if somehow things are still the same as they were before I left? he thought disturbingly, an uncomfortable, cold chill tickling the base of his neck. Tom looked at his house, the front door slightly ajar. *Was that how I left it?*

He started to move toward the house, stiff, jerky movements slowing his progress. He remembered the last time he'd been inside it, seeing again the horrible images of his mother, father, and baby sister locked in the Nacht's embrace.

What if they're still like that?

"What are you waiting for, Tommy?" Abbey Bone cried, and Tom turned to see the little Bone girl starting down the ladder, with Barclay and Roderick waiting to join her.

He was about to share his fears about whether they still might have failed, even after coming all this way, when there was movement before him.

A figure appeared in the doorway, slipping on a pair of heavy work gloves as he prepared for a hard day of harvesting in the turnip fields. Tom craned his neck ever so slightly and saw the shape of his mother behind his father, forever at his side.

"Be sure to leave the door open," his father said, pulling his gloves tight for a perfect fit, "just in case Tom should . . ."

His father saw him first, and the look on his face showed Tom that all his anxiety was for nothing, showed him that all the hardship that he and his friends had gone through, to end up here . . . was a small price to pay.

"Tom," his father said, and Tom had never heard his name sound better, except for when his mother then noticed he was standing there and began to scream it at the top of her lungs, or when his little sister, Lottie, pushed out from between his father's legs, singing out his name in a strange little tune that he was certain would be replaying over and over again — whether he wanted it there or not — inside his head for many years to come.

They ran at him then, and he at them, joining together in a desperate, loving embrace filled with sadness and joy. *So much has changed*, Tom thought as he hugged his family, never wanting to let them go.

But at the same time, so much had remained the same. And he was happy for that.

This was what he had fought for.

Percival had never been much for good-byes and would

have preferred to stay on board the *Queen* as everybody said their farewells before they were on their way.

But the twins wouldn't hear of it, threatening to never speak to him again if he didn't come down the ladder and say a proper good-bye to Tom and his family. He begrudgingly admitted that they were right and joined the group in the yard below.

Abbey was all weepy as she hugged the boy who had become more than a man on their journey to save the Valley.

He'd become a hero.

"Thanks so much for picking us to go on your quest with you," Abbey Bone said, powerfully hugging Tom's waist.

"I couldn't have picked better even if the Dreaming hadn't told me that you were coming," Tom said as he hugged her back.

Barclay was next, sticking out his little hand for Tom to shake.

"Nice knowin' ya," he said, trying to hold back his emotions, but as Tom took the little Bone's hand, Barclay threw himself at the boy and wrapped his arms around him.

"You're one of the best friends I ever had," Barclay said tearfully.

Tom patted the boy's back. "You're one of my best friends, too."

It turned into an all-out crying fest when Abbey and

Barclay had to say good-bye to Roderick, and Percival wasn't sure how much more of this he could take when he saw Tom approaching him.

"They're really going to miss each other," the boy said, watching as the twins and Roderick sobbed in one another's arms.

"Yeah, that's the bad thing about a quest to vanquish evil and stuff," Percival said, feeling himself getting emotional.

"What's that?" Tom asked.

"If you don't get yourself killed, once the mission is over, you have to say good-bye."

"You could stay here," Tom told him with a smile.

Percival knew that he was teasing. "And become a turnip farmer?" He saw that Tom's parents and Randolf — who had been talking with them — were now looking over. "Not a chance," Percival said under his breath, smiling and waving at them. "Think I'd rather clean Roque Ja's litter box."

"Figured as much," Tom said. "No harm in asking, though."

"Nope," Percival said. He was good at adventuring, but this emotional stuff didn't suit him at all. "Well, I guess we should be going," the Bone explorer said.

"Back to Boneville?" Tom asked.

"Yep, eventually," Percival said. "Randolf said that he'd fly with us for a little bit longer, help us with the maps that

I want to draw up before presenting my findings to the Boneville Explorers' Society."

They were both silent then, not wanting to face the inevitable.

"Well, you take care of yourself," Percival said abruptly, turning to grab the rope ladder hanging beside him. "C'mon, kids . . . Randolf. We've got a lot of distance to travel if we're . . ."

Percival was just about to put his foot in the first rung of the ladder when it hit him like a tidal wave. He released his grip, turned back to the boy and rushed into him with a powerful hug.

"You take care of yourself, kid," the Bone explorer said. "If the *Queen of the Sky* ever needed a copilot, it would most assuredly be you."

Tom returned the hug with equal affection until Percival broke his hold, sniffing a bit and wiping at his watery eyes.

"Allergies," he said, sniffing once more. "Must be something in the air."

Tom wiped his eyes, too. "Must be," he answered.

The twins said their good-byes all over again before finally scrambling up the ladder and onto the deck. Randolf was next, promising to see Tom again someday, before heading on up.

"You take care of yourself, Tom Elm," Percival said, and before his allergies could get the better of him, climbed up the ladder to his ship. And before the idea of becoming a turnip farmer started to look good, he got behind the controls of his ship and piloted her away.

EPILOGUE

Life pretty much returned to normal almost immediately. Each morning, Tom and Roderick rose with the sun to head out to the family's turnip fields to harvest the latest crop.

"I didn't think I'd miss this, but I did," Tom said, pulling a healthy-sized turnip up from the dirt and handing it to Roderick, who brushed the loose dirt from it and carried it to the waiting wheelbarrow.

"So you've given up on the idea of becoming one of Queen Thorn's royal guards?" the raccoon asked, tossing the harvest into the cart with the others they'd picked so far that morning.

"For now," Tom said, stopping to rest and staring out at the woods that surrounded their fields. "But one can never tell what the future holds."

He thought he saw something moving in the dark patches of forest and squinted his eyes to see better. He thought he'd seen something peering out at him, something with eerily burning eyes nestled in a face made entirely of shadow, and upon realizing that Tom could see it, it quickly darted away.

"One can never tell what the future holds," Tom repeated, getting back to harvesting the turnip crop. He kept his eyes on the darkness, a true hero ready for anything.

Sitting by the fire that he'd made with a little bit of Dragon spit (it was just about all he could muster since finishing the quest, and he had to wonder if this would be permanent), Stillman sat, thinking about the future as Porter snored away within his shell.

The little turtle was exhausted from their journey, and Stillman had started to feel guilty about not accepting a ride in the sky ship, but he'd hoped to be contacted by the Red Dragon sometime on their journey back. That had yet to happen.

He'd just about given up on that idea when they stopped to rest. Stillman had done what he'd been told, and that should've been enough.

The little Dragon reached behind himself for the stack of twigs that they'd gathered to feed the fire, when a much larger stick was laid in his hand.

"Hey, kid," said the voice that he immediately recognized as the Red Dragon's.

"Hello, sir," Stillman said, climbing quickly to his feet, trying to hide his excitement. "I didn't hear you approach."

"Don't sweat it," Red said. "But we might want to keep our voices down," he suggested. "Don't want to wake your turtle friend." The Red Dragon moved deeper into the woods, away from the fire, and motioned for Stillman to follow. "You done good, kid," Red said with a nod. "Really helped pull our butts out of the fire, so to speak."

Stillman beamed proudly. Praise from the Red Dragon was something that one didn't take lightly. The little Dragon wished now that they had awakened the sleeping Porter, so that he could have heard what the Red Dragon just said to him, but the old Dragon wasn't quite finished yet.

"So, what's next?" Red asked.

Stillman didn't know what he was getting at. "Excuse me, sir?"

"What's next for you?" the Dragon went on. "I see one of two possibilities."

Stillman listened intently.

"You can return with me to the Western Mountains, to sleep with the other Dragons . . ."

Stillman didn't like the idea of leaving Porter behind, but . . .

"Or," the Red Dragon continued, "you could return to your home in the woods with your friend and wait."

"Wait?" Stillman asked. "Wait for what, sir?"

The Red Dragon smiled slyly. "Wait until we need you again. The Dreaming needs agents that it can trust, and just because the Nacht was defeated this time, doesn't mean that the forces of darkness won't attempt to get one over on us again in the future."

Stillman couldn't believe his ears. Me *as an agent of the Dreaming?* It was more than anything he could have ever hoped for.

"So," the Red Dragon said, "what's it going to be? Sleep, or be permanently on call?"

And, watching the Red Dragon's smile match his own big, Dragon grin, Stillman knew he didn't have to speak his choice aloud.

The first map was coming along nicely.

It was early morning over the Valley, and Percival had awakened before the twins and Randolf to review what had been drawn the day before and what was on the agenda for today.

The Bone explorer felt a tingle of excitement pass through him like electricity as he looked at the nearly completed map, thinking about what the Society's reaction would be. They would know that the Bone cousins weren't lying. And Percival could lead an exploratory expedition back to this wonderful place.

Percival couldn't help but grin at the potential for fame

and fortune that awaited him, but first he needed to finish the maps.

He considered making some noise to wake up Randolf, but then thought better of it. After all he'd been through with the quest — after what all of them had been through — a little extra shut-eye would probably do them all some good.

Percival started rolling up the map when he thought he heard something and stopped to listen.

"Hi," came the voice again, and for a minute he thought he was hearing things, when his eyes fell on a tiny bug perched on the *Queen*'s steering wheel.

A tiny green bug.

"Did you just say hi to me?" Percival asked, amused.

"Yep, I did," answered the bug, and Percival just about spit.

"You're a bug," he said, pointing to the little guy.

"I'm Ted. Who might you be?"

"I'm Percival F. Bone," he said. "I'm an explorer, adventurer, and inventor."

"I knew it!" Ted the bug exclaimed.

"You knew it?" Percival asked, confused. "How would you know that?"

"Because they said you would come," Ted said. "That once you knew that they were missing, you would come to find them."

Percival felt that odd, twisting feeling start to form in the pit of his belly.

"Who said that I would come to find them?"

"Your brother and his wife," Ted said. "Norman and Emmy Bone."

Percival gasped, the thought of maps and his return to Boneville for fortune and glory suddenly of no importance. The smell of a whole new adventure, like a coming storm, strong in the wind.

THE END

JEFF SMITH was born and raised in the American Midwest and learned about cartooning from comic strips, comic books, and watching animated shorts on TV. After four years of drawing comic strips for The Ohio State University's student newspaper and cofounding Character Builders animation studio in 1986, Smith launched the comic book *BONE* in 1991. Between *BONE* and other comics projects, Smith spends much of his time on the international guest circuit promoting comics and the art of graphic novels. Visit him online at www.boneville.com.

TOM SNIEGOSKI is the *New York Times* bestselling author of more than two dozen novels, including The Fallen, a teen fantasy quartet that was adapted into an ABC Family Channel miniseries, and the Billy Hooten: Owlboy books. He also collaborated with Jeff Smith on *Tall Tales*. With Christopher Golden, he coauthored the OutCast series, which is in development as a film at Universal. Sniegoski was born and raised in Massachusetts, where he still lives with his wife and their French bulldog, Kirby. Visit him online at www.sniegoski.com.

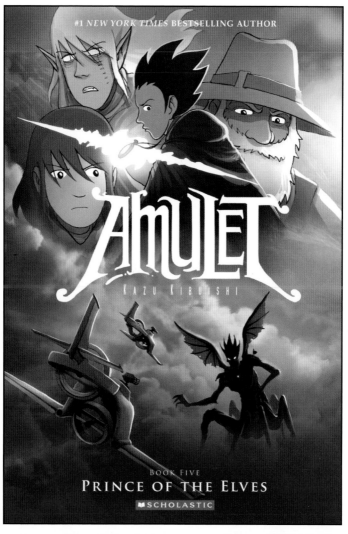

Places, everyone! Raina Telgemeier, creator of *Smile*, is back with her new graphic novel!

What happens to a middle school play when the stage crew and actors aren't getting along, ticket sales are down, and two cute boys enter the mix? DRAMA!

#1 *New York Times* bestseller and Eisner Award winner!

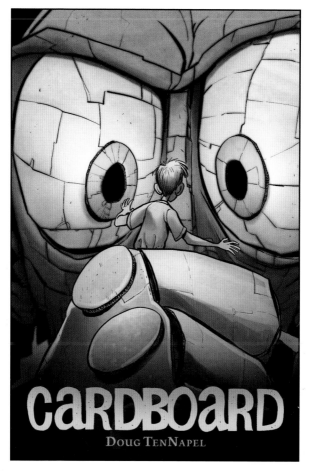

Chickenhare: half chicken, half rabbit, 100% hero!

What's a chickenhare? A cross between a chicken and a rabbit, of course. And that makes Chickenhare the rarest animal around! So when he and his turtle friend are captured and sold to an evil taxidermist, they've got to find a way to escape before they get turned into stuffed animals!